CHRIS PLATT

star gazer

Ω
PEACHTREE
ATLANTA

Ω

Published by
PEACHTREE PUBLISHERS
1700 Chattahoochee Avenue
Atlanta, Georgia 30318-2112
www.peachtree-online.com

Cover design by Maureen Withee
Book design by Melanie McMahon Ives

Printed in June 2011 by Lake Book Manufacturing in Melrose Park, Illinois, in the United States of America
10 9 8 7 6 5 4 3 2 1
First Edition

Library of Congress Cataloging-in-Publication Data

Platt, Chris, 1959-
  Star Gazer / written by Chris Platt.
     p. cm.
  Summary: Thirteen-year-old Jordan's new horse Star Gazer has been neglected and has a lot to overcome, but nevertheless Jordan vows to beat Star Gazer's former owner in the state championships at the end of the summer.
  ISBN 978-1-56145-596-6 / 1-56145-596-2
  [1. Horses–Fiction. 2. Horses–Training–Fiction. 3. Determination (Personality trait)–Fiction.] I. Title.
  PZ7.P7123115St 2011
  [Fic]–dc22
                            2010052068

For all of those who have had the pleasure of working with Heavy Horses.

And, especially to Sheri, Nick, Dani, and Sue,

with special thanks to Sheri Spanial and Sue Vilardi for the technical help and the hours of fun while driving drafts.

one

L ook out!" Jordan McKenzie reached for the dashboard to brace herself. Her mother jerked the steering wheel hard right, making room for the speeding vehicle that had ignored the No Passing sign.

A boy about Jordan's age leaned out the window of the beat-up red truck, laughing and pointing.

"He almost hit us!" Jordan exclaimed. She thought she recognized the kid, but she couldn't be sure. She and her mom had only moved to this town two weeks ago. The vehicle had passed too quickly to see the driver.

"You're *never* getting your driver's license," Jordan's mother said. Her hands were shaking as she guided the car back onto the narrow two-lane road.

"Mom..." Jordan rolled her eyes and blew a stray lock of her dark wavy hair off her forehead. "I'm only thirteen. I've got two more years before I can even get my permit."

Her mother adjusted her rearview mirror and took a steadying breath. "They passed us on a blind curve," she pointed out. "What if someone had been coming from the opposite direction? Or what if a farmer had pulled out with a big piece of heavy equipment? Those boys wouldn't have stood a chance. And they could have killed someone else, too!"

Jordan shook her head at the stupidity of it all, then turned her attention to the scenery. For the last half-hour, they'd been passing through mile after mile of cornfields. Someone had told her that "knee-high by the Fourth of July" was the mantra of every corn farmer in the area.

After growing up in Los Angeles, moving to a farming community in Southern Michigan was quite a change. It was going to take some serious getting used to. But she had never fit in with big-city life anyway. While her classmates in L.A. were wearing makeup and heels, Jordan had been more comfortable in jeans and tennis shoes. Everyone she knew there had all the latest electronic gadgets. Jordan didn't even own a cell phone.

The small township of North Adams, Michigan, where they now lived, was nothing like where she grew up. She'd been used to giant malls and restaurants on every corner. Here, you had to drive thirty miles to get to the nearest McDonald's or Walmart.

Weird.

Jordan smiled to herself as they moved beyond the corn-fields and came to an expanse of soybeans and wheat. *No more cement,* she thought. *No more skyscrapers.* But there were plenty of wide-open spaces and—best of all—horses!

Jordan had wanted a horse of her own ever since she could remember, but even if they could have afforded to buy a horse, it had cost too much to board one in Los Angeles. She'd had to content herself with riding lessons at one of the stables on the outskirts of the city.

The first thing on her list after unpacking the rest of her belongings was convincing her mom to let her get a horse.

For the past couple of years, Jordan had saved her allowance and the money she made from odd jobs. She had almost a thousand dollars in her savings account. She didn't know how much a horse cost in this part of the country, but she was willing to work until she had enough money to buy one.

They passed a two-story brick farmhouse with a hand-lettered sign out front that said, "Fresh eggs and baked goods for sale." Jordan marveled at the antique farm equipment and old-fashioned buggies that stood beside the large barn.

North Adams and the surrounding towns were home to a few Amish and Mennonite families. Jordan wasn't exactly sure what being Amish or Mennonite meant, other than belonging to a certain religion. But she'd learned to recognize these people from their dress and customs. She'd seen an occasional horse and buggy around town, and noticed several groups of women selling baked goods from small booths on the side of the road. With their plain blue dresses, caps that covered their hair, and white aprons, they looked different than the other women in North Adams.

Jordan knew what it was like to be different. She hoped to fit in better here than she had in L.A.

They drove past another large farm. Her mother was driving slowly now, so Jordan craned her neck to get a better look. The name Miller appeared on the mailbox.

She pressed her nose against the window, staring at the two beautiful Belgian draft horses a teenage boy led from the barn. Their golden coats and white manes and tails gleamed in the sun.

Something about those horses had drawn Jordan in the first time she'd seen them on parade in her hometown. The owner of the fancy hitch wagon and team had given her a ride, and Jordan had instantly fallen in love with the unique animals. She was fascinated by their huge size and muscle power. They were twice as big as the horses she'd ridden during the lessons in California. She could see herself owning a draft someday. But they were probably pretty expensive. Jordan flopped back into the seat and sighed. Someday...

They came to the last big curve in the road before their house. Jordan's mom slowed the car even more to make the sharp bend.

"Oh, no!" Mrs. McKenzie slammed on the brakes and pulled off the two-lane road.

Jordan stared at the scene before them, not quite sure what she was looking at. Long black skid marks marred the blacktop ahead. It took her a second to realize there was an overturned vehicle on the side of the road—a red one like the one that had passed them a mile back. The black heap in the middle of the two-lane road was what was left of an Amish buggy.

In the next instant, Jordan noticed a horse lying in the road, partially buried beneath the buggy and tangled in the harness and wreckage. She couldn't be sure if the poor animal was dead or alive.

Her mother threw open the car door and stepped out. "Stay here, Jordan. Use my cell phone and call 911. Tell them there are injuries."

Jordan watched her mother sprint away from the car. She didn't know her mom could move that fast. She took a deep breath and steadied her hands, then dialed 911. She kept her eye on the horse as she pressed the emergency numbers and waited for the operator to answer. She rehearsed what she would say; she knew the name of the highway, and she knew they couldn't be more than a mile from their house. When a woman's voice came on the line, she quickly gave her the information.

By the time Jordan hung up, several other cars had pulled over, and two men were cutting the horse free of his harness. The animal lifted its head and began to struggle, thrashing about on the pavement as it tried to stand.

Jordan sucked in her breath. She was glad the horse was alive, but she hoped it wouldn't cause even more damage to itself than the crash had. Unable to stand it any longer, she shouldered the door open and stepped out of the car.

Her mother came running back toward their vehicle, and for a second Jordan thought she was in trouble for getting out of the car.

"Jordan, grab the first aid kit and follow me."

She retrieved the white plastic kit from the backseat and ran to join her mother. Her heart jumped wildly in her chest. She'd never been this close to an accident.

Jordan took in everything as fast as she could. The troublemaking boys had climbed from their overturned vehicle. They were able to walk, but blood covered their faces and lacerated arms. The older boy limped to a rock and sat down so people could tend his wounds.

The horse was now standing. Jordan couldn't tell how badly it was injured.

Jordan's mother took her hand and dragged her to a spot where an older man and a teenage boy sat on the side of the road.

These had to be the people from the buggy. The elderly gentleman with the long gray beard looked like he'd just stepped out of another century and into the present. A broad-brimmed black felt hat sat at a precarious angle on his head. His dark trousers were torn in several places, and his white shirt and dark vest were stained with blood.

The boy looked dazed. He was dressed like the Mennonite boys she'd seen in town. A big bump showed through the sandy-brown hair on his forehead, and his torn clothing exposed numerous cuts and scrapes. Blood stained his plain blue shirt, and his pants were covered with dirt.

As Jordan looked closer at the old man, she could tell by the pain on his face and the way he held his arm that it might be broken. He stared into the distance and kept up a steady stream of barely audible words that sounded like a foreign language. He tipped his head toward the boy, indicating that Jordan and her mom should take care of him first.

Her mother opened the first aid kit and quickly introduced herself as she began to attend the boy.

He winced when she applied antiseptic to a cut on his arm. "My name is Jacob," he said, "and this is my friend, Brother Samuel Fisher."

She nodded to the older man, then turned back to the boy. "Hold on, Jacob. I'm almost done here," she said. "I'm Mary McKenzie and this is my daughter, Jordan."

"Thank you, Mrs. McKenzie…Jordan." As the boy repeated her name, he gave Jordan a small, pained smile.

Jordan smiled back. Her name sounded different when he said it.

"Do you go to school here, Jacob?" Mrs. McKenzie asked. "We're new in town, and my daughter will be attending junior high here in North Adams this fall."

"Yes, ma'am, I'll be in the same school."

Mrs. McKenzie passed the bottle of antiseptic to Jordan. "You finish up with Jacob, while I see to Mr. Fisher."

Jordan took over, trying to dab on the medicine without causing Jacob too much pain. "Why does Mr. Fisher keep talking under his breath?" she asked. "What language is that?"

"It's called Pennsylvania Dutch," he explained. "It's a German dialect spoken by Old Order Amish. He's asking the

6

good Lord to help the boys who caused this—and praying for patience for himself so he doesn't wander over there and whup their hides."

Jordan paused with the cotton swab in midair, her eyebrows lifted in confusion. "But I thought...?"

"What?" Jacob laughed. "That the Amish don't ever get mad?"

Jordan nodded, feeling heat creep into her cheeks. It *was* a stupid generalization.

"Amish—and Mennonites like myself—are dedicated to a lifestyle of peace and nonviolence," Jacob said, the corner of his mouth turned up in a crooked grin. "But we're human, too. The same things that make you mad are probably the same things that upset us. We just try really hard to control our anger. There's usually a way around violence."

Mrs. McKenzie had finished stabilizing Mr. Fisher's arm. "I wish more people lived by that rule," she said, looking over toward the boys from the red truck.

Sirens sounded in the distance. "Looks like help will be here in a minute," she said. "Once you're at the hospital, they'll take better care of your arm, Mr. Fisher."

Jordan looked surprised. "The Amish can ride in cars?"

Jacob sighed and stood up. He was at least a head taller than she was, and his eyes were a startling blue.

"Yes," he said. "The Amish can ride in cars. They just don't believe in *owning* them. And they don't turn to stone if they walk into a hospital. That's permissible." He tipped his hat, then knelt to speak to his elderly friend.

The older man assured Jacob that he was all right, then looked up at Jordan and her mom. "I'm grateful for your help," he said in his heavily accented English. He turned toward the scene of the wreck. "*Ach*, I need to see about my horse. He's a good animal, *ja*. He didn't need this trouble."

"I'll go check," Jordan volunteered. She needed to get away from this boy and his smiling eyes and teasing ways. And she truly wanted to see how the horse had fared. The men who had freed the animal were more than happy to hand the broken reins over to her. Jordan could tell they knew nothing about horses—not that she was an expert by any means, but she knew a bit more than they did.

"That's a good boy," Jordan said, rubbing the horse's neck to comfort him. While she stood there, trying to decide what to do, the police and ambulance pulled up to the scene, their sirens blaring and lights flashing. The noise caused the old horse to jump around at the end of the reins, despite his injuries.

"Easy, easy," Jordan crooned, placing a calming hand on the horse as she tried to avoid getting her toes stepped on by dancing hooves. Jordan breathed a sigh of relief when the EMTs finally turned off the obnoxious noise and the horse settled down. She decided to move him further down the road away from all the noise and confusion.

Mr. Fisher never got a chance to see how his horse was doing. The medics whisked him and Jacob into the ambulance and sped away. The second ambulance to arrive took care of the boys from the truck.

When the dust cleared, Jordan was left standing at the side of the road, still holding the reins. Her mother joined her and patted the old horse's head. "Looks like we're going to have a visitor for a few days," she said.

"Really?" Jordan couldn't believe her ears.

Her mother nodded. "After I gave the policeman my statement, I tried to ask him about the horse, but he had to move on to the other people," she said. "We can't leave him here by the side of the road. We're not too far from our house. If he can walk, get him heading our direction and keep him off to the side of the road so you're safe. I'll drive behind you with my safety lights flashing."

Jordan turned the horse and started walking toward their new home. It didn't matter that he belonged to someone else and would only be with them for a day or two. They were going to have a real live horse in their barn!

two

Jordan spoke encouragingly to the horse as they walked along the shoulder of the road. The old gelding grunted and had a bad limp, but she thought he'd probably make it to their house okay if they took it slow. She could tend to his cuts and scrapes once she got him home. If things looked really bad, maybe her mom would ask a veterinarian to come look at him. She was sure that's what Mr. Fisher would want.

She fell into step beside the old bay horse. Every now and then he tugged at the reins, asking to stop and crop grass. If her mother hadn't been traveling behind them in the car with her flashers on, she might have given in to his begging.

She studied the horse as they walked. He had a long neck and body, and an angular head. Jordan wasn't sure what breed he was, but he looked rather sad with that long face.

When they reached their house, Jordan led the horse down the slight hill to the back of the property where the rickety old barn stood. She waited for her mother to park the car. "What do we do now?" she asked. "There aren't any stalls set up in the barn and most of the fences have a break in them."

Her mother walked to the barn and pulled on the big door. It squealed in protest, then began to move slowly on the pulleys. Dust and cobwebs floated on the air, disturbed from their usual spot by this unexpected visit.

"I remember seeing an old halter and rope in here when I was exploring," Mrs. McKenzie said, entering the barn. "Maybe we could tie him to the hitching post for a bit while we fix him a place to stay?"

Jordan squinted over at her mother in surprise. "Mom, the only thing we've ever built was a prefab birdhouse. Do you really think we can build a decent stall?"

"We can give it a good try," she called from the interior of the barn. "Ah, here it is!" Jordan's mom emerged victoriously with a faded blue halter and rope in her hand. She handed them to Jordan. "Honey, you're going to have to do this part of it. It's been a long time since I've put a halter on a horse."

Jordan gently removed the bridle, being careful not to bang the bit on the old horse's teeth. She quickly slipped the dusty halter over the gelding's head. "What should we call him?" Jordan said, finger-combing the horse's tangled mane. "We don't know his name, but we've got to call him something—especially if he might be with us for a day or two."

Her mother thought for a moment. "Seems like the Amish would prefer simple names for their horses."

"I think I'll call him Bob." Jordan laughed. "It's a simple name. And did you see the way he bobs his head when he walks?"

"Well, then, why don't you tie *Bob* to the hitching post," her mother suggested. "I'll find something for him to eat. There are a couple of broken bales of hay in the back corner. They look pretty old, but I think they're still good. While

Bob's munching on hay, we can change our clothes and find something to doctor those cuts with. That huge scrape on his hip has got to be painful. I don't see anything that needs stitching, but we still might have to call the vet."

"Can we afford that?" Jordan knew money was tight. The move from California had taken most of her mom's savings.

Her mother paused. "Mr. Fisher would probably take care of the bill. If not, I'm sure we can work something out. Bob needs a vet, and we can't let him suffer."

"I have my savings," Jordan said. "We can use some of that if we have to."

Her mom smiled. "You keep your savings, Jordan. I know how hard you've worked to get it. We've got to make sure Bob is okay, then get him back to his owner as soon as possible."

"Maybe they'll let us keep him for a while?" Jordan said hopefully.

Her mother frowned. "Jordan, don't even go there," she warned. "He doesn't belong to us, and you know we can't afford a horse right now. I was lucky to find a job—such as it is—as quickly as I did."

Jordan sighed as she tethered the old horse to the rail outside the barn, but her mood brightened when she looked at old Bob. She'd make the best of the short time he was here. This was going to be fun!

Jordan ran to the house and changed clothes. On the way out, she raided the medicine cabinet for any supplies she could use to help old Bob. She grabbed some antiseptic ointment, Betadine scrub, cotton balls, and gauze pads. She stopped at the garage and picked up a wash bucket and sponge, then headed back to the barn.

The bay was nibbling on some hay when she got there. His ears flicked back and forth at the sound of her unloading the medical supplies. Jordan could tell by the way Bob shifted his weight from leg to leg that he was in pain.

Her mother brought a few more medical supplies she'd found. "I called a veterinarian, just in case." She set down some old Ace bandages—leftovers from her workout days— and pulled her shoulder-length brown hair back in a rubber band. "His name is Dr. Smith. He'd already heard about the accident—news travels fast around here. He said it was a miracle Fisher's old horse had walked away from it."

"That's for sure," Jordan agreed.

"The vet was very nice," her mom said. "He volunteered to examine Bob for free and said he'll get here as soon as he's able. In the meantime, we're supposed to start treating Bob's wounds."

Jordan picked up the wash bucket and squeezed in a lit-tle Betadine and some soap. "I should have gotten warm water while I was in the house." She frowned at her lack of planning.

"That's okay." Her mother grabbed the bucket and carried it to the hose. "It's been pretty warm today. The water that's been sitting there in the hose has been heating under the sun all afternoon."

Jordan grinned. "You mean we've got solar power now?"

Her mother laughed. "Yeah, I guess you could say that. This will give us at least half a bucket of warm water to work with. Now, let's get busy. I'll call the hospital later and let Mr. Fisher know we have his horse."

They started on Bob's face, washing the cuts and scrapes, then moved down his neck to his withers, back, and sides. Jordan noticed that patches of hair were missing from his hide where he'd been knocked to the pavement when the truck hit the rear of the carriage.

The horse flinched in pain every time they hit one of those spots. Jordan tried to be as tender as possible. Her heart ached for the poor animal, and her anger rose toward the two arrogant boys who had caused this damage. She hoped they had to go to jail—or at least got grounded for life!

She thought about Mr. Fisher and Jacob and hoped that they were doing well in the hospital. She wondered if Jacob would come with the elderly man to pick up his horse.

"You've been standing there holding that sponge for a long time," her mother said. "Where is your mind wandering?"

Jordan didn't want to meet her mom's eyes. "Nowhere," she said and quickly bent to wash the old horse's legs. Her mother gave her an odd grin, but Jordan ignored it and focused her attention on the horse and away from silly daydreams.

"What do you think will happen to the two boys who caused the accident?" Jordan asked.

"I don't know," her mother said. "But it was lucky that no one was killed." She shook her head. "I don't understand how they can let a horse and buggy go right down the same road with vehicles. It seems so dangerous for the buggies," she said. "But one of the ladies at work said the court determined that their buggies have a right to be on the road, too, as long as they have signals on them."

Jordan scrunched up her lips, thinking. Life here was so different. She'd seen horses pulling carriages in other towns. But they were for tourists to use in designated areas, and they moved very slowly. They weren't going down the same road as cars that were driving fifty miles per hour.

They finished caring for the horse, and Jordan's mom turned to toss the dirty water under a nearby elderberry bush.

"I guess we should get started on that stall so Bob has a place to stay. I'd rather not leave him tied to the post all night."

Jordan ran up to the house to find a couple of hammers and some nails. This was going to be quite an experiment. Between her mother's carefully manicured fingernails and Jordan's total lack of carpentry skills, they were in for an interesting time.

But two hours later they had created a stall that seemed pretty solid—strong enough to hold old Bob, at least. They scattered some of the straw they'd found in the loft of the barn, tossed a flake of fresher-looking hay into the corner, and then turned the old bay loose in the stall. Jordan went in search of something to use as a water bucket for Bob while her mom watched the horse munch his hay. By the time she returned, Bob was lying in the deep bedding, almost asleep.

"He's had quite a day," Mrs. McKenzie said.

Jordan nodded. She rested her chin on the top of the stall door and sighed. "Even though he's not ours, it feels good to have an animal here on the farm. It seems...*right.*"

Her mom thought for a moment. "Yeah. There were always lots of animals around when I was a kid," she said. "They're a lot of work. Maybe one of these days we can talk about getting a dog or something. But, you're right, it does feel good to have old Bob here."

Surprised at her mom's answer, Jordan quickly pounced on the opportunity. "Maybe we could get some farm animals?" When she saw her mother about to disagree, she quickly added. "We could start with something small, like a goat, or some chickens. They wouldn't cost much to feed. You know that livestock auction we pass on the way out of town? Maybe we could look there someday?"

Her mother picked up the hammers and the box of nails.

"Don't push your luck, Jordan. For now let's just worry about getting Bob fixed up and back to his owner. I'm heading to the house to start dinner."

Jordan watched her mom walk from the barn. She sighed. How was she ever going to talk her mother into letting her have a horse when she couldn't even convince her to buy a couple of stupid chickens?

three

Jordan got up early the next day to take care of Bob. His wounds were looking better already. As she changed the old horse's bandages, she wondered how Mr. Fisher and Jacob were doing. Maybe her mother would call the hospital later and get the news. She finished dressing Bob's wounds and gave him breakfast, then made her way back to the house. She wanted to get started on her other chores right away. It was already muggy, and their house didn't have air-conditioning.

Pushing open her bedroom door, Jordan stared at the clutter. An assortment of boxes and crates stood stacked against her bedroom wall. They'd been there for the past two weeks and she couldn't bring herself to unpack them.

At thirteen, Jordan was starting a brand new life—for the second time. The first change had come two years ago when her father had left—just up and walked away like he was stepping out of an old pair of shoes. And now, here was major life-change number two, life in a small town after growing up in a humongous city.

She leaned on the paint-chipped windowsill and looked out her window. The old farmhouse where they now lived had once belonged to her grandmother. Without this place, they wouldn't have had anywhere to go when their money ran out in L.A.

They hadn't seen her grandmother very often in recent years, but Jordan remembered visiting here a couple of times when she was very young. Her crayon drawing of a horse still showed through the thin coat of paint on the closet wall. She smiled to herself. Even back then, she had known that she wanted a horse.

Mary McKenzie entered the room, heels clicking smartly on the old wooden floor. "Honey, those boxes aren't going to unpack themselves," she said, searching through her battered purse for her car keys. "I've got to run to the hardware store for some screws to put up that big shelf in the living room. How about getting some of them unloaded before I get back?"

Jordan said goodbye to her mom and reached for the closest box. Sitting cross-legged on the floor, she lifted out some books and a small reading lamp and placed them on the floor beside her.

A soft knock sounded on the door. Her mother must have forgotten something. "It's open," Jordan said, pulling some horse statues from the box.

"Hi!" A cheerful voice called from the doorway. A tall, dark-haired girl stepped into the room.

Jordan's head jerked up in surprise.

"I'm Nicole Wilson. I live right down the road," the girl said with a nervous smile. "Your front door was open. I hope it's okay? I guess I'm kinda like the welcoming committee or something." She held out a plate of chocolate chip cookies.

"Uh, hi," Jordan stammered as she got to her feet and dusted her hands on her jeans. "I'm Jordan." She moved forward awkwardly—were they supposed to shake hands, nod heads or what? How did they do things in these small towns? Somehow a big hug just didn't seem appropriate in a situation like this.

Jordan smiled and reached out to accept the plate of cookies. "Mmmm, my favorite," she said, lifting the plastic wrap. She offered one to the other girl before taking one for herself.

Nicole took a nibble of her cookie. "I'm sorry I didn't get here right when you guys moved in, but my mom had me on restriction because my final grades were pretty bad." She brushed cookie crumbs from her shirt. "But I spent the past two weeks in a special tutoring session the school offered, so now I'm free for the summer."

Bad grades were something Jordan had never had to deal with. They'd called her bookworm and teacher's pet at her old school because she studied a lot and got decent grades. It had been another thing that set her apart from the others. Maybe she wouldn't let this potential new friend know about that part just yet.

"Want some help?" Nicole offered, pointing to the boxes.

Jordan took another cookie before setting the plate on the nightstand. "Thanks for offering, but that's okay." This girl seemed nice enough, but it would feel odd having someone she didn't know digging through her private possessions. Besides, she didn't want to scare off a new friend by boring her to death with unpacking.

The sound of a horse whinny echoed from the front yard, and Jordan paused with her cookie mid-bite. She hoped Bob hadn't gotten loose from his stall.

Nicole laughed. "That's my horse, Dakota," she said. "I tied him to your tree. I hope you don't mind?"

First Bob, and now another horse? How lucky can I be? she thought. "Can I see him?" Jordan asked. Before Nicole had a chance to answer, Jordan was already making her way to the front door.

She sucked in her breath when she saw the little black horse tied to their apple tree. "He's beautiful!" she exclaimed as she hurried down the front steps, Nicole at her heels.

"Dakota's a Morgan gelding," Nicole said proudly. "He's eight years old and a lot of fun to trail ride. Sometimes I show him in the summer and fall. There's a big riding stable down the road, and a bunch of girls that go to my school board their horses there." Nicole paused and weighed her words. "They're kind of snobby and have really fancy horses, but they can be a lot of fun. Did you have a horse where you came from?"

Jordan slowed her steps when she approached the gelding. She knew better than to run up on horses and startle them. "No, I came from Los Angeles," she said. "There wasn't any room for a horse at our place and it cost too much to board one there. The only pet I've ever had is a goldfish named Petey."

Jordan reached out to pet Dakota. His sleek coat was so soft. She closed her eyes and inhaled his warm horse scent while she stroked his neck. "I took some riding lessons while we lived there, but I didn't get to go very often. There's nothing I want more than to have my own horse. This looks like perfect horse country. I'm hoping I can talk my mom into it soon."

"Yeah, you need to get a horse so you can go riding with all of us," Nicole said. "Do you want to ride Dakota around the yard right now? He's very gentle."

Jordan glanced down the road. She badly wanted to ride the little black gelding. But she had chores to do, and she needed to stay on her mom's good side if she was going to talk her into a horse. "I'd love to," Jordan said. "But my mom will be home soon and I'm supposed to get those boxes unpacked." She smiled apologetically. "Maybe sometime soon?"

Nicole nodded. "Sure, that would be great." She glanced around the property. "You've got plenty of room here. If you fix a few fences, it'll be perfect for a horse."

Jordan smiled. "That would be awesome." She gave Dakota a good scratch on the neck, chuckling at the way his lips moved as if he were begging for more.

Nicole untied Dakota and mounted up. "I'm glad you moved into the neighborhood. Maybe I can come over again soon? You can tell me all about Los Angeles and your family and I'll fill you in on our small-town gossip." She grinned and turned her horse toward the road.

Jordan watched her go, wishing she had taken Nicole up on her offer to ride Dakota. Maybe if Bob got better before they came to pick him up, she could ride him? She hurried back into the house. She wanted to come up with a good plan to convince her mom they needed a horse. But first, she had to get all those boxes unpacked.

* * *

"Here they are, Mom." Jordan pulled a small box of one-inch screws off the shelf at the combination hardware/ furniture/ ice cream store. The screws her mother had purchased earlier in the day were too short, so they had brought them back to exchange.

Jordan looked around the small-town store. North Adams wasn't big enough to support certain businesses on its own, so folks took to combining their space to accommodate the locals and make a living. The small market where her mother had gotten a job also ran a real-estate office out of its back room. It was a big change from the clothing company she'd worked for in L.A., but it was a job.

She followed her mother to the counter and waited for her to pay for their merchandise.

"Thank you," Mrs. McKenzie said to the shop owner. She handed the bag to Jordan and shouldered open the door while she dug her keys from her purse. "Let's go home and get dinner started."

Jordan settled into the car and fastened her seatbelt. "Pizza?" she asked, remembering the frozen pepperoni pizza she'd seen in the freezer.

Her mother pulled from the parking lot onto the main road. "Ah, yes, pizza…the number one food of all growing teenagers."

"Yup." Jordan laughed as she rolled down her window. The open window worked just as well as the air-conditioning in their old car. Her mother called it their "two-forty air-conditioning"—you roll down two windows and drive forty miles per hour. Jordan smiled as she let her hand play on the breeze. Southern Michigan seemed hotter and muggier than Los Angeles. Maybe because of all the local lakes and greenery around here.

She turned to her mother. "So, this girl came over today while you were gone."

"Oh? Who?" Her mother rolled down her window, too.

"Her name is Nicole, and she lives down the road from us," Jordan said. "She has a horse."

"Uh-huh," her mother mused, lifting her brows.

"She's going to come back and visit again," Jordan said, trying to figure a way to bring up the subject of getting her own horse. Maybe she should tell her mom having a horse would help her make some new friends. But no, it would probably be better just to come out and ask. Her mother had always told her that if she wanted something, she needed to stand up and state her case. But she really hated hearing the word "no." And besides, that rule only went for standing up to *other* people, not her mom.

"I assume Nicole is going to bring her horse over?" Jordan's mom asked.

Here was her chance. Jordan took a deep breath and plunged right in. "Mom, we're in the perfect place now to have a horse. I've got almost a thousand dollars saved."

"I know, honey," her mother reached over and patted her knee. "But even if you used your savings to buy a horse, how would we pay for the hay and the upkeep? Your father didn't leave us with much when he left, and as you know, the move wasn't cheap."

When they pulled into their driveway, Jordan was pleased to see Nicole waiting on their front porch. The girl smiled and waved as they got out of their car.

"Hi, I'm Nicole." She stepped forward and shook Mrs. McKenzie's hand. "My mom said to give you this since Jordan and I ate so many of the cookies I brought over earlier." She handed her a homemade coffee cake. "It's my mother's specialty."

Mrs. McKenzie accepted the gift with a smile. "Why, thank you, Nicole. That's very kind. Please tell your mother I appreciate it." She motioned for Nicole to follow them inside.

Nicole took a seat at their kitchen table. "I just heard you guys helped out the people in that wreck yesterday. I bet that was something."

Jordan was surprised. She didn't think many people in

town knew them. "How'd you hear it was us?"

Nicole grinned. "Welcome to the small-town grapevine. Our internet connections might not be very fast, but word-of-mouth travels *very* quickly around here."

Jordan had already heard about the local grapevine, but she didn't realize just how fast it worked. In Los Angeles, you were lucky if you knew the name of someone the next block over after living there six months. Here, it seemed everyone in the town knew everybody else's business right away. She wasn't so sure that was a good thing. She pulled out the chair next to Nicole and sat down. "Who were the boys that caused the accident?" Not that Jordan would know them, but she was curious.

Nicole pulled her hair up off her neck and fanned herself. "The younger one was Tommy Sutton. His family owns that big Percheron farm on the edge of town. His dad is a VIP here in town. He won't let anything happen to his son. The other kid is from two towns over. I don't know him, but I hear he's sitting in jail right now."

"Good," Mrs. McKenzie said as she placed a glass of ice water in front of Nicole and poured some for herself and Jordan. "I should call the hospital and see how poor Mr. Fisher and Jacob are doing."

Jordan blushed a little at the mention of Jacob's name. Nicole gave her a questioning glance and Jordan quickly looked away.

"Jacob has always gone to public school," Nicole said, studying Jordan's face for a reaction. "Some of the Mennonite families in this area homeschool, but Jacob and a few others go to North Adams schools."

"He seemed like a very nice boy," Mrs. McKenzie said, smiling at Jordan.

Jordan quickly changed the subject. "We're still taking care of Mr. Fisher's horse," she told Nicole. "Did you bring Dakota with you today? I was telling my mom about him."

Nicole took a sip of her water. "No, it's his dinnertime, so I left him home." She turned to Jordan's mom. "I'm hoping Jordan can get a horse soon so she can go riding with me."

Mrs. McKenzie glanced over at her daughter. "Well, that might be rushing it a bit, Nicole. We only moved in a few weeks ago. A horse is a big responsibility—and a big expense."

Jordan frowned. It was the same speech her mom had given her earlier. "I'm trying to talk my mom into going to the local auction house and buying some chickens or a goat or something," she told Nicole. "But she's not too keen on that idea, either."

Nicole seemed to sense Jordan's need for some backup. "Yeah, my neighbors raise miniature goats. They're really cute, and easy to take care of. And if you got chickens, you could have fresh eggs for breakfast."

Mrs. McKenzie mulled the idea over for a few seconds. "You know, when I was little, my mother used to have a hen house. It was right out there between the barn and the house. I loved helping her gather the eggs," she said nostalgically. "Yeah, maybe a few chickens would be good to start. We'll see about the goat later."

"There's a livestock auction coming up this Saturday," Nicole suggested. "My parents take me to it sometimes. This auction has everything, and it's a lot of fun to watch. Maybe you guys could go with us?"

Mrs. McKenzie looked at her daughter, who had on her most hopeful face. "I'm sorry, honey, but I've got to work this weekend."

Jordan tried really hard not to show her disappointment,

but she could feel her lips settling into a hard line. Going to the auction with her new friend sounded like so much fun.

Her mother hesitated. "Well…maybe if I arrange to meet Nicole's parents and make sure all these plans are okay with them, then *you* could go." She took out a knife and cut a thin slice of the coffee cake Nicole had brought. "That would give me a chance to thank them in person for the welcoming gift." She took a bite of the cinnamon-and-sugar-laced cake. "Mmmm…" she said through a mouthful of the tasty treat. "This is wonderful!"

"Really, Mom?" Jordan said. "You'd let me go?"

Her mother nodded as she cut several more slices of the coffee cake. "Anyone who can make a cake this delicious has *got* to be good people." She handed Jordan and Nicole each a piece. "I think it's nice that you can make new friends here and have someone who lives close by to hang out with, Jordan. And, I think I'm warming up to the idea of fresh eggs for breakfast."

"Awesome!" Jordan said. "We'll make the arrangements for you guys to meet."

Mrs. McKenzie put the cake away before she wrecked everyone's appetite. "We'd love to have you stay for dinner, Nicole."

"Thanks, Mrs. McKenzie, but my mom's expecting me home. She's teaching me how to make lasagna tonight."

"Oh, sounds yummy. Be sure to bring us a sample, okay?" She laughed. "If it's as good as this cake, I think *I'll* be your new best friend."

Jordan walked Nicole out onto the front porch and slapped her a high-five. "All right! We're going to the auction!"

Nicole looked her straight in the eyes and grinned. "I couldn't help noticing that look on your face when your mom talked about Jacob. You like him, don't you?"

Jordan blew out an exasperated sigh. "It's no big deal. I don't even know him. I only got to talk to him for a few minutes after the accident."

"This town is pretty small," Nicole said. "I'm sure you'll run into him again. My dad tells me to stick to Dakota and forget about boys." She laughed. "Is your dad strict?"

Jordan shoved her hands deep into her pockets and stared out over the cornfields. "My dad walked out on us two years ago," she said softly.

"Whoa…" Nicole just stood there, embarrassed that she'd put her new friend on the spot. "I'm really sorry, Jordan. I shouldn't have been so nosy."

They stared at each other in awkward silence, then Jordan spoke up. "It's okay. It's *his* loss. He doesn't get to see what a great kid I am," she said, laughing at her own humor.

Truth was, Jordan tried not to think about how much *she* had lost in the whole process.

She walked Nicole down the porch steps. "We're friends now, right? So if we're going to be hanging out together, I guess that's a part of my life you should know about."

Nicole gave her a quick hug. "Sometimes dads do some really stupid things. It's not your fault. Maybe someday he'll wake up and see what a fool he's been."

Jordan nodded, then shifted to a lighter mood. "Okay, enough seriousness. Let's concentrate on getting to the auction and buying some chickens so I can move on to bigger and better things—like a horse!"

"I think it's a good sign that your mom's letting you go to the auction with us." Nicole smiled and headed toward the road.

Jordan waved goodbye. For now it was just chickens, but she was sure it was the first big step toward getting a horse of her own!

four

The next afternoon, Jordan was cleaning Bob's stall when she heard someone enter the barn. Her mother came forward with a big smile and a handful of carrots. The old horse eagerly stretched his neck and extended his lips, trying to grab the treats before they were even within reach.

"You're right," her mother said, being careful that Bob didn't mistake her fingers for a carrot in his haste to gobble the treats. "It is good to have an animal around the farm. Truth is, even though they're not really what I consider pets, I'm really looking forward to getting those chickens."

Jordan finished with the cleaning, and let herself out of the stall. "We can get more than just chickens, Mom. Nicole says there will be lots of animals at the auction: cows, goats, horses, pigs…"

Her mother shook her head. "No, I think I want to start small, then maybe we can work our way up to a lamb or something later on."

"Okay," Jordan said, wondering if she'd ever be able to talk her mom into getting a horse. "Baby goats and potbellied piglets are *really* cute, though," she said. "What if I come home with one of those?"

Her mom fed Bob another carrot. "If you come home with *anything* more than chickens, you're grounded." She gave Jordan the Mom Look. "I mean it," she said.

Jordan breathed a sigh of disappointment. She knew her mother meant every word.

A soft tap sounded on the barn door and both their heads snapped up in surprise. They weren't expecting visitors.

"May I enter?" a voice called from the doorway.

Jordan's stomach did a little flip when she saw Jacob step into the dim light of the barn. His blond hair gleamed in the one shaft of sunlight that sliced through the broken board at the side of the barn. She was uncomfortably aware that she had on her old, baggy sweat pants and a wrinkled T-shirt. They seemed so shabby compared to the boy's simple, clean, and neatly pressed clothes.

"Carrots, huh?" Jacob said. "You're going to spoil this horse so much that he won't want to go home."

"Well, hello, Jacob," Jordan's mom said. "You found us. I wasn't sure if my message had ever reached Mr. Fisher in the hospital."

"He got it." He held out a piece of stale bread and the gelding took it, munching happily. "Also, Dr. Smith called my father and told him that the horse was okay and where to find him. Brother Fisher asked us to come over here and fetch him."

"How's he doing?" Mrs. McKenzie asked.

Jacob ran a hand through his thick hair and frowned. "They kept him there a couple of nights for observation and X-rays. They were afraid he'd fractured his pelvis, but it turns out he's only got a small break in one of the bones in his lower arm. It isn't all that serious, but he won't be driving Ned any time soon."

"*Ned* is this horse's name?" Jordan could tell Jacob was trying not to laugh. "We've been calling him Bob. And he eats
bread? I didn't know horses liked bread."

Jacob offered Ned another piece. "It's made from grain.
A lot of horses won't eat it, but some of them develop a taste
for the stuff. Brother Fisher doesn't like to see anything go
to waste, so he puts the stale bread in his pockets and feeds
it to the horses and birds."

He let himself into the stall and put the halter he'd
brought with him over Ned's head. "He said to thank you for
taking care of his horse, and for helping us after the accident."

"It was our pleasure," Mrs. McKenzie said. "Would you like
me to follow you home in our car? That's how we got Ned
back to our place. How far from here do you live?"

Jacob smiled. "Thank you, but that won't be necessary. My
dad brought our horse trailer. He's waiting out front." Jacob
looked directly at Jordan, playfully daring her to ask if Amish
horses were allowed to ride in trailers.

Jordan kept her mouth shut. She now knew that there
were big differences in the way Jacob's Mennonite family
lived and the traditions of the Amish community that Mr.
Fisher belonged to. She wanted to learn more, but she
refused to let the boy lead her into asking more questions.
He'd just think she was a dumb city girl. He almost looked
disappointed when she didn't rise to the bait, and the
thought made her smile.

"Jordan, why don't you go with Jacob and help him load
Ned?" Her mother shooed her toward the door.

She gave her mother a quit-playing-matchmaker look.

Jacob glanced over his shoulder. "Come on, Jordan. I'd be
happy for some help."

She hesitated, then decided to go. She'd never had a chance to load a horse into a trailer before. It would be a good learning experience. And that, she told herself, was the *only* reason she was following the tall blond boy.

Ned stumbled a bit going up the slight incline to their driveway, where a big white truck and horse trailer were parked. Jacob put a steadying hand on the old horse's neck and spoke words of encouragement to him.

When they reached the trailer, Jacob introduced Jordan to his father. She shook hands with Mr. Yoder, who stood several inches shorter than his son. He wore a straw cowboy hat and had a closely trimmed beard. Jordan instantly liked his kind smile.

"It was good of you and your mother to take care of this old horse," Mr. Yoder said. "Samuel's wife sent something for you." He walked to the cab of the truck and pulled out a box, which he handed to Jordan.

The warm, yeasty smell of freshly baked bread wafted from the box. "Mrs. Fisher is known for her bread and her rhubarb pie—a specialty of many of the bakers in this area."

"This is awesome!" Jordan said. "Please thank them for me, Mr. Yoder."

"You can call me Mr. Yoder if you're more comfortable with that, but everyone around here calls me Leroy. I'll be sure to relay your message." He opened the door to the trailer and nodded for Jacob to load the horse.

As soon as Jacob tossed the lead rope over Ned's neck, the old horse walked straight into the trailer on his own.

"Well," Jordan said, "I was a lot of help."

The boy grinned sheepishly. "You needed to come get the bread anyway. And it gave me a chance to talk to you again."

"Come on, Jacob, let's get going," his father called.

Jacob gave Jordan a smile that made her heart quicken. She chided herself for being so goofy. Boys had smiled at her before; what was it about this one that was different?

He made her feel welcome, Jordan thought. That was important when you were the new kid in town.

"I'll see you around." Jacob waved and stepped into the truck.

"See ya." Jordan waved back. She hoped he was right. But the chances of seeing him before school started again were slim. And he'd probably forget all about her by the time school started in the fall.

As they pulled out onto the main road, Jordan wished she had thought to ask what kind of horses the Yoders had. They definitely had a nice rig.

She watched the big truck and trailer until it was out of sight, then headed into the house with the box from Mrs. Fisher. It might wreck their dinner, but Jordan was all for cutting into the rhubarb pie right now. A big piece of bread with jam on it didn't sound too bad, either.

* * *

Jordan spent the next several days checking out the local scene, which had a whole different meaning in Los Angeles than it did here in this cow town. She bought ice cream at the hardware store, and tried to start a conversation with some girls who came in. They were friendly enough, but they seemed to be in a rush to get their cones and go somewhere else. A couple of times, Jordan made an effort to meet the eyes of kids she passed on the street, but most of them just looked at her like she didn't belong. She felt like she had *new girl* stamped in the middle of her forehead. She had better luck with older people, though. If she walked through town in the late afternoon, they'd be sitting on their porches, and they'd always wave to her when she went by.

With Nicole's help, Jordan tacked up signs around town looking for odd jobs, and she soon had a list of several people who were willing to pay her to mow their lawns and weed their flowerbeds. One person called to see if she'd shovel out his cow barn for twenty dollars. Jordan respectfully declined that job.

By the day of the auction, she had almost eleven hundred dollars in her account. Too bad she only had permission to buy chickens with it.

Jordan rose early that morning. The auction didn't start until ten, but Nicole and her parents had said they'd be here to pick her up at eight-thirty. They wanted to have plenty of time to get their bid card and look at all the livestock that would go through the sale ring.

Excitement made Jordan's pulse quicken when they pulled onto the auction grounds. It felt like a whole new world. As soon as they got out of their car, a cacophony of animal sounds greeted them. Cattle bawled as they were moved through the high wooden chutes to sale pens; goats and sheep bleated their concern at being in a strange place. Once she thought she heard a donkey bray. She was most excited, though, when a horse neigh came from one of the barns.

The parking lot was filled with cars, trucks, and trailers of every imaginable description. She saw everything from rigs worth tons of money to homemade contraptions that were no more than several two-by-fours fitted into the back of a pickup to allow for the hauling of smaller livestock.

Nicole's mom and dad steered them toward the registration booth. Jordan people-watched as they made their way through the crowd. Most of the auction-goers were farmers, but a few looked more like city folks. One man in a suit and tie looked totally out of place. Jordan wondered if she also stood out as a city slicker. She hoped she could just blend in with the farmers.

Several Amish families had set up booths and were selling garden vegetables, freshly baked pies and breads, and homemade jams. Other booths displayed handmade leather goods, such as bridles and harness. She looked for Mr. Fisher, but didn't see him.

"Let's get our bidding number, then we can go look at the animals," Nicole's mother said. "Jordan, would you like to have your own bid number? I know you're buying chickens for your farm. You can have your own card if we sign for you."

Jordan hesitated. "Um, sure, Mrs. Wilson. That would be great."

Jordan and Nicole followed her mom to the registration office, where they had to stand in a long line. The girls chatted and fidgeted, anxious to be off exploring the auction grounds. Ten minutes later, they weren't much closer to the front of the line. Nicole begged her parents to let her take Jordan to see the animals.

"Oh, all right," Nicole's mom said with a laugh. "Go explore the sale barns. We'll catch up with you two as soon as we're finished here."

"That way," Nicole said, pointing the way to the sale barns.

The first one they came to had a dozen stacked cages of chickens and turkeys. Jordan looked them over carefully and decided she liked the black-and-white speckled hens the best.

"Poor turkeys," Nicole said. "They fill up the entire inside of their cages. I wonder if my parents will let me buy one?"

A concerned neigh sounded and Jordan immediately lost all interest in the chickens. "Let's go!" she said. They followed the direction of the sound to the pens behind the barn. Several Quarter horses stood in a large area eating hay. A couple of auction workers answered questions, while another man haltered a horse for a buyer's inspection.

The two girls hung around for a while watching the horses, then Jordan told Nicole she wanted to check out the chickens one last time.

Nicole waved her on. "I'll meet you inside. My parents always sit in the third row."

Jordan nodded and hurried toward the poultry cages. The muggy heat of summer was bearing down, and she decided to detour through the next barn to get out of the sun.

A soft nicker drew her attention when she entered the barn. Jordan looked around but didn't see any horses. The stalls in this section held mostly goats and pigs. There were signs everywhere asking people not to enter the stalls. Jordan imagined a stampede of goats or pigs caused by someone forgetting to latch a stall door.

When she heard a rustling sound from a stall several yards away, she went over to see what was there. It took a moment for her eyes to adjust to the darkness. Jordan was surprised to see a large, black draft horse standing in the back corner with its head hung low.

Jordan leaned over the stall door, attempting to get the horse to move forward. She couldn't tell if it was a mare or a gelding, but whatever it was—even in the dark stall—she was sure it was beautiful!

"Come here, baby," she crooned. The horse flicked its

ears, but remained where it stood in the gloomy corner of the stall.

She *had* to see this horse. Already she sensed something wrong, the way it stood in the shadows like it didn't want to be bothered.

Jordan stepped back and looked up and down the aisle. There were a few people at the other end, but no one in the immediate vicinity. She eyeballed the Do Not Enter sign. Then she took a deep breath, flipped the latch on the door, and walked into the stall.

five

Jordan stood there for a moment, sure the horse and any person within twenty feet could hear the banging of her heart against her ribs. Stepping into a dark stall with a very large horse she didn't know wasn't a very smart move on her part. There was a good reason for the Do Not Enter signs on the stalls. What if the horse suddenly charged her?

She was about to back away when she heard the soft blowing of the black horse's nostrils as it tried to catch her scent. "It's okay, pretty one," Jordan said softly, sizing up the large animal. She took a careful step forward and waited for the horse's reaction. The big horse flicked its ears back and forth at the sound of her voice and the crunch of the straw under her feet.

Jordan took another step and held out her hand for the horse to sniff. The horse stretched its thick, arched neck, touching its muzzle to her hand. The soft, warm breath tickled Jordan's palm and she let out a loud giggle. Startled, the horse pitched its head high in the air.

"Easy," Jordan said, noticing that the beautiful animal had a large white star in the center of its forehead. She reached up and touched the horse's muzzle, which was still raised rather high. "Everything's okay," she murmured. The draft lowered its perfectly shaped head and Jordan stroked the white spot between the horse's eyes. "Aren't you gorgeous!" she said in awe, and the horse lowered its head even more, nudging her gently with its nose.

A minute later, footsteps sounded outside the stall and Jordan held her breath, hoping she hadn't been discovered. She backed deeper into the shadows and tried to make herself as small as possible. If she got caught, she'd embarrass Nicole's parents, and her own mom wouldn't be all that happy to find out that she'd disobeyed the rules.

"I think there's someone in there," a man said as he poked his head into the stall and peered around. "Go in and check, would you, please?"

Jordan's stomach did a double flop when the latch slid open and the door creaked. She was busted!

A tall boy walked into the stall, staring into the shadows before he spoke. "Jordan...? What are you doing here?"

The voice sounded very familiar. "Jacob?" Jordan asked. Even though she had wanted to see him again, part of her hoped it wasn't him. How could she explain being in the stall with a huge draft horse when the sign outside clearly warned Do Not Enter?

Jacob held his hand out. "Come on, Jordan. Get out of there. Didn't you read the sign? This mare outweighs you by about two thousand pounds."

Jordan let him take her hand and lead her out of the stall. "The horse wasn't dangerous," she muttered, humiliated that she'd been caught breaking the rules. She hoped they didn't boot her out of the auction. Not only would she be in a lot of trouble, but she also wouldn't be able to bid on those pretty chickens she'd found.

Jacob closed and latched the door. The mare stepped from the back corner and walked to the center of the big stall, her ears pricked in their direction. Jordan thought she noticed a bit of a limp in the horse's step.

"Hmmm…she must like you," Jacob said. "That's the most interest she's shown in anything since they brought her in." He took off the flat-brimmed straw hat and brushed back his hair. "Have you been here before?" he asked, putting his hat back on.

"Umm, not really," Jordan said. "How about you?"

Jacob grinned. "Yeah, I kinda work here. My dad's the auctioneer."

That announcement got Jordan's attention. She'd never been to a live auction, but she'd seen auctioneers on television and wondered how they could talk so fast. Most of the time she had a hard time figuring out what they were saying.

Now that she knew Mr. Yoder was the auctioneer, she felt even worse about breaking the rules. He'd been kind to her. But Jacob didn't seem too upset, so maybe it wasn't such a big deal. "That's pretty cool," she said. "I bet it's fun working here."

"It beats sweeping floors," he said. "It's a lot of hard work, but you meet a lot of interesting people and animals."

"What do you mean?" Jordan cocked her head, interested.

Jacob leaned on the stall door. "Every person and animal here has a story. Take this mare, for instance." He plucked a piece of hay from the rack and twirled it between his fingers. "Her name is Star Gazer. She's a registered Percheron mare and is from Gilbert Sutton's Farm. She used to belong to his daughter, Karina. She named her Star Gazer after her favorite pastime."

At the mention of the Sutton name, Jordan's ears perked

up. "Wasn't his son one of the boys who caused the accident with you and Brother Fisher?" she asked.

Jacob nodded.

At the moment, Jordan didn't like Gilbert Sutton very much. She stared at the large black mare with the white star and frowned. "This horse is beautiful. Why would anyone want to get rid of her?"

"I'm not sure. They say she used to be one of Sutton's best skidding mares."

"What's a skidding mare?" Jordan asked, sure that the question would just make her seem even more ignorant.

Jacob didn't seem to find anything wrong with the question. "Around here we have a log-pulling contest at the fair every year. They call it *skidding*. You hook up a team of horses and pull a set of logs through some obstacles without touching or moving any of them. It's a timed event. Gilbert Sutton has won it the past four years in a row. He's pretty proud of that."

"Did Star Gazer ever win one of those contests for Mr. Sutton?" Jordan asked.

Jacob thought for a few seconds before answering. "I believe she did. But when Karina went away to school a few years ago, the mare missed her so much that she lost all interest in pulling."

"That's so sad," Jordan said. "Star Gazer must have really loved her owner. She's missing her best friend." She felt her throat tighten and quickly pushed those sad thoughts aside.

Jacob nodded. "I know. Animals have feelings, too. Once Star gave up on pulling loads, Mr. Sutton didn't have any use for her. He's got a lot of really good brood mares already, so he shipped her off to auction."

"He just threw her away?" Jordan was appalled. Her heart ached for the abandoned mare. No wonder she had felt drawn to her. "Who would get rid of such a beautiful animal? Couldn't Mr. Sutton find some other use for her?"

"That wasn't the only problem," Jacob said. "This mare is lame in her front feet. My dad looked at her, though, and he couldn't find anything wrong other than some problems with her hooves. They're really short and badly chipped. Dad said that might be why Mr. Sutton is unloading such a nice mare."

"How much will a horse like this bring at auction?" Jordan asked.

"It's hard to predict," Jacob answered. "But I'd say she should bring somewhere around eighteen hundred dollars. It all depends on who's here and how badly they want the animal."

Star Gazer took several more gimpy steps and stuck her head over the door, pushing her nose at Jordan again. Jordan felt the velvety softness of her muzzle and laid her cheek against the side of the mare's head. Star smelled of hay and horse and long rides across the fields on a warm summer day.

Jordan sighed. It would be a dream come true to own this horse. If only Mr. Sutton had waited a few more months to send her here. If she'd had time to save more money, maybe she could have talked her mother into letting her buy the big draft horse. But for now, she was just here for…chickens. "I hope someone nice will buy her," Jordan said, her heart squeezing at the thought of not being able to take this magnificent creature home with her.

Jacob's brow furrowed. "I doubt it. Not with the packers here," he added as if he expected Jordan to know what that meant.

"Packers?" she asked.

Jacob's eyes widened in surprise. "You don't know about the packers?"

Jordan shook her head.

"Never mind then. Forget I said anything." He turned and walked down the barn aisle. "Enjoy the auction. I'll talk to you later."

Jordan frowned. He sure had cut the conversation short. Why would…? Suddenly, she understood. "Wait a second," she said, running down the aisle after Jacob. She grabbed his sleeve before he could get away. Jacob wouldn't look her in the eye, and Jordan knew her suspicions were right. "She's going to be sold to a place that will put her in a dog food can, isn't she?"

Jacob nodded. "Probably, but you never know, someone might buy her for a pet."

Jordan felt sick. "How can they let those buyers come in here?"

Jacob shrugged. "We can't keep them from coming to the auction. They get to bid just like everyone else. I know it seems like a bad thing to a lot of people. But if an animal is too old, or sick, or broken down, there's not a whole lot you can do. It's sad, but it's a fact of life."

"But what about the ones that are fine and healthy?" Jordan shoved her hands into her pockets and kicked at the ground, sure that she wasn't going to like the answer to her question. "They can buy healthy animals, too?"

"Yeah," Jacob nodded. "That's the part I don't like. If there's no one in the audience willing to outbid the packers and buy a healthy horse, then the unlucky animal will go to the same place as the sick or injured ones." He patted Star on the neck. "Let's just hope there's someone here who wants to buy her and take her home to spoil her."

star gazer

Jordan's shoulders slumped. She wished *she* could be the one to buy the mare. When she looked into the gentle brown eyes of the beautiful draft horse, she felt like crying. She reached out and straightened the horse's long forelock. Star Gazer needed rescuing, but there wasn't a thing she could do to help.

six

There you are," Nicole said, making her way down the barn aisle toward Jordan. "And I see you found Jacob." She pointed toward a stall at the end of the row, where he stood helping a customer.

"You *knew* he worked here and you didn't tell me?" Jordan squeaked.

"I wanted it to be a surprise." Nicole tossed her hands in the air and shouted, "*Surprise!*" She hiked her purse onto her shoulder and smirked. "I hope you two had a nice little conversation."

"Ugh!" Jordan smacked her palm to her forehead. "Jacob caught me in a stall with a horse."

"Which stall? Which horse?" Nicole asked, amused at the situation even though Jordan looked like she wanted to crawl into a feed bin.

Just then, Star poked her head over the stall door and nuzzled Jordan's hair.

Nicole jumped. "Oh, my, I didn't see you!" she told the horse, then turned to Jordan. "You mean *this* horse? *Right here?* With the big Do Not Enter sign over its head?"

Jordan nodded as she stroked the draft horse's neck. "That would be the one," she said sheepishly.

"Well, they haven't booted you out yet, so I guess you're probably okay," Nicole said. "And...you got to see Jacob again."

Star Gazer nuzzled Jordan once more and she happily turned her attention from the embarrassing encounter with Jacob back to the horse. "Isn't she beautiful?" Jordan brushed her hair back into place. "Her name is Star Gazer."

She waved the flies off the horse's face. "Jacob said she came from the Sutton farm. Mr. Sutton didn't want her anymore, so he just threw her away." She stared into the mare's eyes, her heart aching for the big black mare. "I wish I could buy her, but Jacob says she'd probably go for around eighteen hundred dollars. I just wish I'd had another year to save up."

"She is pretty...in a big, clunky sort of way," Nicole said. "But what would you do with her? You don't have any harness or a cart or wagon. If this mare came off the Sutton place, she's a pulling horse."

"I could ride her," Jordan said, looking up at the height of the mare's back. Dakota would seem like a pony beside her.

Nicole started to laugh, but changed her mind when she saw that Jordan was serious. She came closer, standing next to the horse. The draft mare towered over them. "That's a long way up there, pal. Won't that be scary being so far off the ground?"

Jordan thought about it. She hadn't had that many riding lessons, and the horses she'd ridden had all been fairly short. Maybe her friend had a point. "I'd find some good use for her," she said, defending herself. "She deserves better than being hauled to the auction just because someone didn't want her anymore." She stood silent for a moment, listening to Star Gazer's steady breaths. "Jacob says the packers might buy her."

Nicole stared at Jordan in disbelief. "Are you sure? My dad said he'd heard a rumor that the packers had a guy who bought stock at this auction. He said the guy doesn't always buy just the sick or injured ones either. I didn't believe it."

Jordan frowned. "He'd probably be careful not to let anyone know who he is. Somebody might decide to get revenge or something."

"Did Jacob say he knew for sure that a packer was going to buy this horse?"

"Not exactly. But he said it was a good possibility."

"That would be horrible," Nicole said, shaking her head. "What are you going to do?" she asked. "Do you want to use my phone to call your mom? I bet she'd let you buy her if you told her she's going to be sold for dog food."

Jordan frowned. "Even if my mom said I could buy her, I still don't have enough money."

"Well, it's not a done deal yet." Nicole put her arm around Jordan's shoulders, lending sympathy for the bad situation. "There's still a chance that someone could buy her and give her a great home." She steered her toward the exit. "Let's get back to our seats. My parents want to buy some lambs that'll be going through the sale ring right away. My mom has your bid card. You'll need it for your chickens."

Jordan followed Nicole down the aisle, careful not to look back. She didn't want to see those big brown eyes begging for someone to take her home and save her.

When they got to the poultry cages, Jordan sent Nicole ahead to their seats while she took one last look at the chickens. A small crowd had gathered. There were several families and a few older men looking, too, trying to decide which ones they wanted to bid on.

One man in particular caught Jordan's attention. He was

star gazer

short and stout, with a bald head and a corncob pipe stuck between his teeth. He pulled bits of grain out of his pocket and fed it to the turkeys while making gobbling sounds. The big birds answered him back and everyone laughed.

When an announcement came over the speaker system warning the auction was about to start, the onlookers moved on.

Jordan remained by the chickens for a few more minutes, trying to decide if she also wanted one of the funny-looking hens with the big fluffy feathers on their legs. As she stepped forward, the toe of her shoe hit something. She looked down and saw a brown leather wallet lying in the dirt.

She picked it up, wondering who could have dropped it. Since it was right in front of the turkey cages, she thought of the funny little man who had gobbled with the turkeys. Glancing around quickly, she spotted him just leaving the barn and ran to catch him.

"Excuse me, sir!" She jogged to his side and stopped. "Is this your wallet?"

The man reached to check his back pocket. When he discovered his wallet missing, he took a closer look at the one Jordan held out to him. "Well, I'll be…" He flipped it open and showed his driver's license photo to Jordan. "You've got the right guy, and I thank you very much, young lady. Can I give you a reward for being honest? A lot of people wouldn't have returned a wallet."

Jordan shook her head. "Thank you, but that's okay. I'm just glad I found you." The man smiled his thanks and walked off, and Jordan headed to the sale ring to join Nicole and her family.

Jordan had thought it was noisy in the sale barn, but that was nothing compared to the auction area. Not only was everyone talking amongst themselves as animals were brought into the ring for the bidding, but there was also the constant banging and clanging of metal gates as each set of pigs or cows was brought through to the viewing pen.

And on top of it all was the voice of Jacob's dad, Leroy Yoder, blasting through the speaker system with his singsong auctioneer chant, telling buyers where the current bid stood. Prices went up and up until there was only one bidder remaining. Then the auctioneer pounded his gavel with a resounding *crack* as he hollered, "Sold!" At that moment the highest bidder owned whatever was on display.

"This is really exciting!" Jordan said, taking her seat next to Nicole. "I can't wait to bid on the chickens. I found a couple of sets that looked pretty good. "

Fifteen minutes later, a cage with three speckled hens was brought in. The chickens ran about the cage, flustered from all the noise and attention. From his spot in the auction area, Jacob caught Jordan's eye, then gave a nod in their direction, indicating that these chickens would be a good buy.

Her pulse raced as she got ready to make her first bid. She leaned forward on the edge of her chair.

"Are you going to be okay?" Nicole's dad asked. "I can bid for you if you want."

"Thanks," Jordan said. "I think I can do it."

As soon as the chicken cage was placed on the platform in the center of the ring, Jordan snatched the bid card from her lap and stuck it in the air, waving it about excitedly.

The microphone crackled. "We love the enthusiasm, miss, but we haven't started the bidding yet." Mr. Yoder winked in their direction.

Jordan felt her face grow hot, but she laughed along with the rest of the crowd. When the bidding finally started, she jumped right in with her card raised. He heart pounded with excitement as spectators took turns running up the bid.

When the gavel fell, Jordan was the proud owner of three speckled hens. She'd paid ten dollars apiece for them. She wasn't sure if that was a good deal or not, but she thought they were worth every penny.

"That was so much fun!" she said. "Where are those chickens with the fluffy feathers on their legs? I want to bid on them, too."

Nicole's mom laughed. "Whoa, better slow down a little bit," she cautioned Jordan. "I think you've got a touch of auction fever. If you're not careful, you'll be going home with a gaggle of geese and a bunch of potbellied pigs."

"Bring 'em on!" Jordan joked, and they all had a good laugh.

A flock of sheep were herded into the ring, and Nicole's parents prepared to bid. Jordan let her mind drift back to Star Gazer. She crossed her fingers, hoping some nice person in this crowd would buy the big mare.

She scanned the faces, wondering if the packer was in the crowd. Her eyes lit on a tall, thin man with a hawk nose. He stood near the entrance to the sale arena, carefully watching the livestock that came through. Jordan wasn't sure what a packer would look like, but that man seemed to be the most likely candidate. Maybe she could distract him somehow when Star Gazer came through the pen.

Jacob herded some calves into the ring. The little red Herefords bolted about, confused by all the noise. Some bucked and played, others bawled for their mamas, and one flopped down in the middle of them all like he was going to take a nap.

They waited through another ten minutes of livestock showing, then the door to the sales ring opened. The crowd oohed and aahed as Star Gazer walked into the pen, her head held high and proud, even as she limped on her two front feet.

Jordan sat straight up. Butterflies swirled in her stomach.

"Take a look at what we got here!" Mr. Yoder's voice boomed over the speaker system. "This beautiful and talented mare comes to us from the famous Sutton Farm. She's got a bit of trouble in her two front feet. We're not really sure what the problem is, so this mare is selling 'as is.' Can I get an opening bid?"

A low mumbling rippled through the room, then a shout of "Yep!" went up from someone standing near the back.

"Who is that?" Jordan asked Nicole.

He's one of the spotters," Nicole said. "They listen and watch for bidders that the auctioneer might not see."

"I've got five hundred!" the auctioneer shouted. "Do I hear six?"

Jordan quickly glanced over at Jacob to see if he knew who had made the bid. The look on the boy's face told her everything she needed to know.

The wrong person was bidding on Star Gazer.

seven

Jordan's world tilted as the bid quickly rose to six hundred dollars. "Who's bidding?" Nicole's mom asked, craning her neck to look.

"The bad guy and at least one other person," Jordan said, still trying to see where the bid had come from.

Nicole squeezed her mother's hand. "Mom, we think it's a packer bidding on her. They're going to put her in a can if we don't do something."

Nicole's mother shook her head in disgust. "I wish there was some way to keep those people out of here."

"I have six hundred, looking for seven," Mr. Yoder chanted.

Jordan picked up her bid card. "I've got about one thousand dollars. I've got to do something," she said, "or Star Gazer is going to die."

Nicole's mom looked alarmed. "But dear, I thought you were only here to buy chickens. Won't your mother—"

"Seven hundred!" Mr. Yoder shouted. "I've got seven hundred, looking for seven-fifty."

The crowd buzzed with excitement, waiting to see who would win the bid.

"I've got to do it," Jordan said, her hand shooting into the air. "I've got to at least try to save her." She waved her card, praying Nicole's parents wouldn't stop her. They'd signed for her card, giving permission for her to bid. They probably regretted it now.

"Lookie here," the auctioneer said in his singsong chant. "This little lady is going from chickens to draft horses." The crowd chuckled along with him. "That's quite a jump there, missy."

Mr. Yoder looked to Nicole's parents to verify that the bid was okay. Jordan figured they must have been stupefied, because they didn't object.

"I'll accept your bid of seven hundred and fifty dollars," Mr. Yoder hollered into the microphone. "Do I hear eight?"

"Oh, dear!" Nicole's mother said as her hand went to her throat. She turned to her husband. "Do you think Jordan's mother is going to be okay with this? Should we stop the bid?"

In the time it took Nicole's dad to respond, the bidding went up another one hundred dollars.

"Mom, Dad, we've got to help Jordan," Nicole pleaded with her parents. "Please let her bid."

"Please, Mr. and Mrs. Wilson, I'll take all the blame and punishment," Jordan begged. "Even if my mom grounds me for a year. I can't let Star Gazer die."

"I have eight hundred and fifty dollars," Mr. Yoder said. "The young lady has been outbid. Would you like to bid nine hundred, miss?"

Jordan didn't dare breathe. She waited for the Wilsons' answer, praying that the hammer wouldn't fall before they gave it to her. If Mr. Yoder banged his hammer before she could give the next bid, then all was lost. Star Gazer would belong to the packer.

"Mom...Dad...you've got to decide now!" Nicole said.

Mrs. Wilson nodded. "Go ahead, Jordan. We'll figure something out when it's all done." She shook her head. "But what am I going to tell your mother?"

Jordan raised her bid card as fast as she could. "Nine hundred!"

The other bidder instantly upped the bid to one thousand dollars. They were already at Jordan's breaking point.

Nicole placed her hand on Jordan's arm. Jordan wasn't sure if it was to get her attention or stop her from bidding.

"Whoever you're bidding against, they're not going to stop," Nicole said. "Jacob told you they might go as high as eighteen hundred. You're already at your limit if you bid again. If that's a packer bidding against you, he's got tons of money to work with. He'll just keep running up the bid."

Mr. Yoder continued his auctioneer chant. "I have one-thousand-one-thousand-one-thousand... Can I get eleven hundred?" he added, staring directly at her.

Jordan felt almost as bad as she had the day her dad walked out on them. She couldn't breathe and blood pounded in her ears, making it difficult to hear. She was out-bid and there was nothing she could do about it. She couldn't, and *wouldn't*, ask the Wilsons to become any more involved than they already were.

"Are you in for eleven hundred?" the auctioneer asked.

It pained her to do it, but Jordan had to shake her head.

"One thousand going once...going twice..." He paused, giving them one last chance, then smiled sadly before banging his gavel. "Sold, to bidder number thirty-five for one thousand dollars!"

Jordan looked to Jacob. She had a hard time seeing him through the tears that pooled in her eyes. They locked eyes for an instant and he tipped his head to a man on the rail, indicating the winning bidder. "No...," she whispered. *It couldn't be!*

Standing by the rail was the short bald man who'd lost his wallet. The turkey gobbler! But he'd been so nice. He couldn't possibly be the man who hauled horses to the packer!

Jordan's breath came out in one big *whoosh* and her gut tightened. She swallowed hard, trying not to be sick. She could hear the sighs and booing of the people around her. They wanted her to have the horse, too.

She looked up, trying to catch the attention of the bald man who had won the bid. For the first time, he turned and looked to see who he'd been bidding against. Jordan saw the surprise register on the man's face when he realized who it was. Shaking his head, he left the auction block.

Nicole's mom grabbed her purse. "Well, we gave it a good try," she said. "Let's just pay for our livestock and go." She reached over and gave Jordan a motherly hug. "I don't imagine you want to stay any longer, do you?"

Jordan shook her head and gathered her things. She thought about going back to visit Star Gazer one last time, but knew she'd end up blubbering like a baby. Jacob would make sure the mare was well cared for until the packer loaded her up.

She took a deep breath and tried to smile at the people who gave her a sympathetic look or pat on their way to the payment window, but her heart was breaking. She hadn't been able to save the beautiful mare. She followed the Wilsons, trying hard to stop the tears that threatened to fall.

They had to wait in line for several minutes while the people in front of them settled their accounts. Jordan hadn't felt this miserable in a long time. Her stomach actually hurt. She just wanted to get this over with and go home. Maybe coming to the auction hadn't been such a great idea after all.

"Jordan, wait!" Jacob hollered as he cut through the crowd and ran toward them.

Jordan's head snapped up at the sound of the boy's voice.

When he reached them, he had a big smile on his face. "You've got to come back to the auction ring. The packer told my dad that he'd made a mistake and couldn't take the mare. Star Gazer is going back through the sale ring right now! Since you were the only other bidder at the end, you get the first right of purchase at your last offer!"

Jordan stood there listening to Jacob's words, but they weren't sinking in. "What does that mean, Jacob?" she asked. Her head was spinning, trying to make sense of it all.

Nicole grabbed her by the arms and swung her around to face her. "It means you're going to get another chance!" she said. "Your last bid was nine hundred dollars. Sometimes the winning bidder can't follow through on his offer. When that happens, the next highest bidder is given the chance to buy the animal at their last bid price. That means *you!*"

Jacob motioned them forward. "You need to return to the sale ring and officially tell my dad that you want the bid at nine hundred dollars."

Jordan turned to Mr. and Mrs. Wilson. "Can I?" she pleaded. She'd already lost Star Gazer once. She couldn't bear losing her a second time.

Mrs. Wilson looked to her husband. He gave her a smile. "I guess we're all in this together, Jordan," she said. "Go ahead and make your offer. If your mom doesn't want the horse, then we'll have to take responsibility for her. We'd have to find a new home for Star and try to get your money back, though. We can't keep her ourselves."

Jordan gave them both a big hug. "I'm really sorry that all this happened," she apologized. "I feel terrible that I dragged you into it. I don't usually do things like this. But I can't let Star Gazer die. It's not fair. Her owner shouldn't have abandoned her like this."

Mr. Wilson rounded them all up. "Let's get back to the auction before it's too late."

Jordan walked back into the sales ring and a loud murmur of approval rose from the crowd. Mr. Wilson signaled his approval to the auctioneer, and Mr. Yoder slammed the hammer on the podium with a loud *crack*. "Sold to the chicken lady for nine hundred dollars," he crowed.

The onlookers applauded loudly.

"You did it!" Nicole wrapped Jordan in a big hug. Then she laughed and held her out at arm's length. "What in the world are you going to do with a horse the size of a Volkswagen? You only came here to buy chickens!"

Jacob interrupted them to congratulate Jordan. "Well, it was a crazy ride, but you won in the end." He took off his hat and dusted the brim. "What are you going to do with her?"

Jordan shocked herself by blurting out, "Star Gazer's going to win that log-skidding contest at the fair this year." She wasn't sure what made her say that. She didn't know a thing about draft horses, let alone driving them. But Mr. Sutton needed someone to give him some competition, and Star Gazer would be the perfect horse to do it.

Jacob gave her a doubtful look. "You're biting off a pretty big chunk there," he cautioned. "Are you sure you can handle it? That contest is only a couple months away and you're new to the sport. In fact, you're kinda new to everything."

Jordan felt a bit hurt. Jacob didn't think she could do it. She knew that she'd be the weak link in the process. She was starting from scratch. But she could learn how to work with draft horses, couldn't she?

Jacob seemed to sense that he'd hurt her feelings. "We've never had a girl in the log-skidding contest," he said. "But there's no reason you couldn't give it a try...assuming Star Gazer doesn't have anything seriously wrong with those feet."

He stuffed his hands in his pockets and looked at her. "You've got to face it, Jordan. There's a good chance that Star Gazer might have something really wrong with her hooves. Sutton doesn't just get rid of prime breeding stock. Star Gazer might have to be put down if she's broken any of those bones in her hooves. You need to get a vet to look at her as soon as possible. That's my best advice."

The full impact of Jacob's words hit her like a horseshoe between the eyes. Jordan leaned against the wall and took a deep breath, letting it out slowly. She'd just spent most of her savings on a horse she knew very little about. A horse that was lame and might have to be put down anyway. Maybe she needed to just take one step at a time. "I know," she said. "But for now, I just want to get her home and make her happy."

Jacob nodded. "How are you going to get her home?"

That was a good question. Jordan frowned. How *would* they get the big mare home? Especially with sore feet. She couldn't exactly walk her the ten miles to their house.

"We've got a trailer," Nicole said, "but there's no way Star will fit in it."

"My dad and I could deliver her to you if you can wait until Monday," Jacob offered.

Jordan smiled. "That would be really great. I'm going to need a few days to get the place ready anyway." *That's the understatement of the year*, she thought. They'd fixed the stall up for Ned when he'd stayed with them a few days. But it was pretty flimsy. They'd need to reinforce it and make it bigger to hold an animal Star Gazer's size.

Plus, she'd need the extra time to figure out how to tell her mom that a huge horse was coming to live with them.

Jordan's head was beginning to hurt. What was she going to tell her mother? They were already living on a shoestring budget, and her mom only had plans for raising a few chickens. What would she say when the Yoders delivered Star Gazer?

Jordan knew one thing for sure. She should forget about her plans to enter the pulling contest at the fair. When her mother found out she'd just bought an injured draft horse, Jordan would be so thoroughly grounded, she wouldn't see the light of day for an entire year.

eight

Jacob led them back to Star Gazer's pen. This time, when Jordan stood by the mare, she looked at her through new eyes. Star Gazer was hers! She'd waited for this day for so long—and now it was finally here. She had a horse of her very own!

She placed her hands on either side of Star's head and rubbed the mare's large cheek bones. She almost had to stand on her tiptoes. Everything about this horse was massive. The halter they'd found in the barn definitely was too small. Nothing that fit a normal-size horse would work on Star. Good thing there were a lot of draft horses in the area. She'd seen Amish-made halters in the local tack store. She'd be shopping there soon—right after she mowed a few more lawns.

"Well, I've got to get back to work," Jacob said. "But don't worry about your mare. You took care of ol' Ned for us, so now we can return the favor." He waved and walked away, then turned back, pulling a small pad of paper out of his pocket. He scribbled something on the top sheet, tore it out, and handed it to Jordan. "Here's our phone number in case you guys have any questions or need anything."

He gave her a mischievous grin, daring her to ask him if Mennonites were allowed to use modern gadgets like phones.

Jordan beat him to the punch. "Yeah, yeah, I get it. Mennonites *can* have telephones."

"Hey, now you're catching on," Jacob teased. "Brother Fisher follows the old Amish ways and doesn't own one. But he can come over and use ours if he feels like it." He turned to the Wilsons and tipped his hat. "Have a good day. You guys can check out at the cashiers. Once you've paid for everything, I'll help you load up your smaller purchases."

An hour later, Jordan was sitting on the porch steps with her cage full of speckled chickens. Her mother would be home from work soon. Jordan had gone over every imaginable reason for buying a lame horse. But none of them sounded better than the truth: She'd bought Star Gazer because the mare was going to the killers, and she couldn't let that happen.

Her mother was going to totally flip out.

Jordan's foot tapped uncontrollably on the wooden step and she nibbled at her fingernails. When she heard the sound of a car engine slowing down to make a turn and the crunch of tires on gravel, she burst into tears.

Her mother quickly climbed out of the car and took a seat next to her on the stairs. "Jordan, honey, what's wrong?" She put her arm around her daughter's shoulders and pulled her close. "Why are you crying? What happened?"

The enormity of what she'd done hit home. Jordan choked back a sob. Her mother was going to be so disappointed in her. Mrs. McKenzie tucked a long strand of hair behind her daughter's ear and pulled a tissue from her purse to wipe away the tears. "There now," she said softly. "Calm down and tell me what happened."

Jordan hiccupped. "I didn't mean to, Mom, but I couldn't help myself. They were going to send her to the killers!"

The look on her confused mother's face was so comical, Jordan almost stopped crying. She realized how silly her words had sounded. She sat up straight and took a deep breath. "Mom…I did something that's going to really upset you…"

Her mother tried to put on her I-can-handle-this face. "What did you do, Jordan?"

The chickens clucked and pecked at their cage, filling the silence while Jordan tried to think how to word her story. There was no easy way to put it, so she just blurted it out.

"Mom, I bought a lame draft horse."

Even the chickens stopped clucking. The silence drew out so long that Jordan felt like they were frozen in time.

Jordan's mom tilted her head and her brows drew together. "You bought a *horse?* How did *that* happen?"

Jordan shrugged. "There was this big beautiful draft horse at the auction," she explained. "She was lame and her owner didn't want her anymore, so he just dumped her at the auction and walked away. I knew just how that poor horse felt."

Jordan's mom sat in silence for a minute. She studied Jordan's face and brushed away a few more tears, then let out a deep sigh. "This is about your father, isn't it?" she asked.

Jordan scrunched her lips and looked down at her feet. "I don't know—well, maybe." She felt the tears stinging the backs of her eyes again. She needed to push away the ugly thoughts about her dad. She already felt bad enough about her rash decision to buy a horse they couldn't afford. "The packer was bidding on her and there wasn't anybody to save her, so I bought her to keep her from ending up in a dog food can," Jordan said.

"Where were the Wilsons in all of this?" Mrs. McKenzie asked, the exasperation leaking into her voice. "They were supposed to be watching you."

Jordan frowned. "Please don't blame Nicole's parents, Mom," Jordan begged. "It's all *my* fault. I put up the bid card without asking them, then I begged the Wilsons to let me buy her." She sniffed and brushed away the hair that had stuck to her hot, sticky face. "They said they'd find the horse a good home if we couldn't keep her. They're going to call you later to ask about your decision."

The hens started clucking again and Jordan's mother studied them for a moment before speaking. "You've put us in a bit of a situation here, Jordan. You bought an animal that we can't afford to keep. It was nice of the Wilsons to offer to fix this problem for you, but I can't really ask them to do that. You created this mess, and you are going to be the one to figure it out." She paused for a moment waiting until Jordan nodded in agreement, then continued. "Will the auction take the horse back?"

Jordan shook her head. She didn't want to give Star Gazer back. "The Wilsons already paid for her. I have to pay them back on Monday. That's when Mr. Yoder and Jacob are supposed to deliver Star Gazer."

"I see." Jordan's mom folded her hands in her lap and stared out across the soybean fields.

Jordan knew that look. It pained her to know that she'd caused this much trouble for her mom. "I...I know you're really upset about this, but—" Her mother fixed her with a stare that cut her off midsentence and made her feel like crawling under the porch.

"Jordan..." This calm, steady voice worried Jordan a whole lot more than screaming and shouting. "You went to an auction this morning," her mother continued, "with permission to buy some chickens. You came home with the chickens, *and* the news that you've purchased a draft horse—a *lame* draft horse. Your savings is now gone, and we're going to have to figure a way to feed this horse *and* ourselves. Yes, I am upset."

"But, Mom," Jordan squeaked. "The packer was buying Star Gazer for dog food. Jacob said they like buying the bigger horses because that way they get their money's worth." She searched her mother's face. "I'm sure you would've done the same thing if you'd been there."

"Maybe I would have," Mrs. McKenzie admitted. Her shoulders seemed to sag under the weight of the problem Jordan had caused. "But the problem still remains. We've got a horse that we really can't afford, and if she's lame, there's no way we can sell her—except to run her back through the auction. And then she'd probably just end up in a can anyway."

Jordan gazed into the distance. "I know. I've put us in a pretty big mess," she said. "But if you'll just meet Star Gazer, you'll see why I couldn't let her go to the packers. I'll work and earn some extra money to help care for her."

" All right, Jordan. Here's what we're going to do," her mother said, her tone brooking no argument. "I'll meet Star Gazer on Monday when Mr. Yoder and his son come to deliver your horse. *You* can mow lawns and weed flower beds for the neighbors to help pay for the upkeep on this horse. Then you're going to come home and do a whole list of chores that I have for you. By the time you're done, you're going to have calluses on your calluses. And maybe somewhere in there, you will have learned a lesson."

Jordan was thrilled that her mother was going to let Star

Gazer come home with them. "I'll work until I drop," she promised.

Her mother gave her a don't-mess-with-me stare. "I'm not finished yet," she warned. "We're going to see if we can get this mare healthy again, and then we're going to try to sell her."

Jordan's moment of victory slipped away. But she knew this was as good as it was going to get for now. Her only hope was that her mom would fall in love with the big draft beauty just as she had. She lifted her eyes to her mother's face. "I really am sorry, Mom."

Her mother let out an exasperated sigh and folded her in a hug. "I know you are, dear. Now you can show me just how sorry you are by taking those chickens out to the barn and feeding them. After that you can grab the hoe and start weeding that big flower bed over there."

Her mother picked up her purse and walked into the house, leaving Jordan sitting on the porch steps wondering if she was going to regret her decision to buy Star Gazer.

* * *

The next morning, Jordan was up with the sun. She didn't want her mom to have to ask her to do chores. Jordan swept the kitchen floor and started a load of laundry. Then she put on her old sweats and headed to the barn to give it a cleaning it probably hadn't had in a decade.

The pretty speckled hens clucked and scratched the barnyard dirt, picking at seeds and worms. Jordan had caught her mother smiling last night when they'd turned the hens loose to explore their new home. She just hoped her mom would look as fondly at the new horse.

Jordan stared at the fences surrounding the pasture where

Star would be kept. She had a lot of work to do before the draft mare arrived. All sides of the enclosure had places where boards were missing or broken, and someone had dumped several loads of weeds and garbage that would have to be removed. And her head swam when she thought about everything that needed to be done inside the barn. She wished Nicole was here to help, but her mother had grounded her from seeing Nicole for a week.

She found a bunch of old lumber and some wire stacked in a corner of the barn. Some of it was still good. She could use it to fix a new stall and rebuild some of the fence. It wouldn't look all that great, but she didn't care, as long as it worked to keep Star Gazer in.

Around ten o' clock, Jordan looked up from pulling a broken board off the old fence and was surprised to see her mother coming down the hill wearing jeans and work boots. She had a tool belt cinched around her waist. Her dark hair was tucked beneath a blue polka-dot scarf. Despite the work attire, she looked really pretty. The move from L.A. had been a hardship, but Jordan hoped the country air and slower pace of a small town was doing her mom some good.

Her mother surveyed the work Jordan had done on the fence. She looked impressed. "Not bad. What do you say we start fixing up that stall?"

"Sure," Jordan said. "I'm not very good at this. I'll take all the help I can get."

As the day wore on, it grew muggy and they felt lucky to be working in the shade of the barn. There were enough boards to expand the stall and even make improvements to the adjoining outside corral. Jordan thought they'd even have enough to finish up the pasture fence she'd started.

"We'd better take a break now," Jordan said. "Mr. Yoder

should be here with Star Gazer pretty soon." She stayed behind to check the stall and corral one more time while her mother went to the house to clean up.

Ten minutes later, her mom hollered down the hill that the trailer was pulling into the driveway.

Jordan took off at a run, reaching the front yard just as Jacob and his dad hopped out to unload the horse. Her heart banged wildly in her chest—partly from the run, but mostly from excitement. Star Gazer was finally being delivered!

Mr. Yoder opened the trailer door while Jacob went inside to untie Star and lead her out. There was a lot of banging and clanging as he turned the large mare around and led her out. Star paused at the edge of the trailer, not wanting to take the twelve-inch step to the ground.

"Is she okay?" asked Jordan.

"Yeah," Jacob said. "But her front feet are still pretty sore."

"You might want to get the vet out here and have some X-rays taken as soon as possible," Mr. Yoder added. "You need to make sure there's nothing cracked or chipped on those bones inside the hoof."

Just then, Star Gazer stepped from the trailer, stumbling painfully and almost falling down.

Jordan hurried over and ran her hands calmly over the mare's jet-black coat. "Easy, girl, it's going to be okay."

But deep in her heart, Jordan wondered if it really *was* going to be all right. She'd bought a horse she knew very little about, and it had taken all of her money to do it. How were they going to pay for X-rays? And what if there was something terribly wrong? Star might have to be put down. That would be the saddest thing ever and their rescue would have been for nothing.

She stood there for a minute with her stomach tied in

knots. Tears burned her eyes, but she refused to let them fall. *Things will work out,* she told herself, reaching a shaky hand for the lead rope that Jacob was holding out for her. This was her big dream coming true. Everything had to be okay.

But as she attempted to lead Star Gazer down the slight hill to her stall, doubts as big as the draft mare herself settled in Jordan's heart.

nine

Be careful!" her mother warned as she watched them make their way toward the barn. "I'll be down to help as soon as I'm done speaking with Mr. Yoder."

Jordan took her time leading the Star Gazer down the slight incline. The draft behaved like a trooper, picking her way slowly and carefully down the hill. She touched Jordan gently with her nose several times, and nuzzled her hair.

"I'm happy you're here, too," Jordan told the big mare.

Walking beside Star Gazer for the first time gave Jordan an idea of just how big and powerful this mare truly was. She felt like a tiny Shetland pony walking in her shadow. She was glad they had reinforced the stall.

Jacob walked behind, giving Star a push on the rump when she stopped. "I think she likes you," he said. "She hasn't really been that friendly with the rest of us."

"We're going to be the best of buds," Jordan said, placing a comforting hand on Star's neck as they progressed toward the barn. She kept Star moving at a steady pace, but the mare stumbled several times. "Poor baby," Jordan crooned. "It's just a little bit further, then you can rest in your comfy stall. I made the straw really deep."

"My dad has some Easy Boots we can loan you," Jacob

offered. "They might help Star. I'll ask him if he can drop them off to you tonight."

Jordan looked over her shoulder as she kept the horse moving forward. "What are those?"

"They're hard rubber boots that fit over the hoof. Kind of like tennis shoes for horses," he explained. "They keep their feet off the ground and can help stop the lameness from getting worse."

Jordan sighed. She had a lot to learn about equine medical care. The riding lessons hadn't provided her with any information on health matters. "We probably can't afford to get X-rays right now," she said. "I spent all my money buying Star. What's the best thing I can do to help her?"

Jacob shrugged. "If she were mine, and I couldn't get the X-rays right away, I'd probably pack her feet with some medicine to draw out the soreness. She has heat in her front hooves. That usually means there's trouble."

"Oh," Jordan said, frowning at the thought. She had definitely taken on a project that might be bigger than she could handle. But she had to try for Star Gazer's sake.

"I can bring you some of Brother Fisher's poultice in a day or two, if you'd like. It smells really bad, but it works really well."

"That would be great," Jordan said. "I'll do anything that will help Star. I want her to be happy here."

When they arrived at the barn, Jordan handed Star's lead rope to Jacob so she could open the big door. The shade inside felt cool compared to the heat and humidity that brewed outside.

Jacob waited until Jordan tossed some hay into the manger, then he let Star Gazer loose in her new stall. The mare lowered her head to smell the fresh straw bedding, then went to the manger and grabbed a mouthful of hay. She chewed and watched them between bites.

Jacob leaned on the stall door, looking in. "I saw your friend Nicole at the feed store yesterday," he said. "She told me your mom didn't know you bought this horse. She said you got in a lot of trouble."

He fixed her with a stare from his bright blue eyes and Jordan squirmed beneath the scrutiny. "Yeah, my mom gave me a long lecture and a chore list a mile long. I can't speak to Nicole for a week, either."

"I'd say you got off lightly," Jacob said.

Jordan felt a bit defensive. " I didn't buy Star just to defy my mother."

Jacob laughed. "Lighten up, girl. I just meant that my parents probably would have punished me a bit harder if I'd done something like that." He took off his hat and ran a hand through his hair. "Look, Jordan…I know your heart was in the right place and you wanted to save Star. But I hope you realize how serious all this is. These drafts are big, powerful horses. And from what you tell me, you haven't been around horses that much. I hope you haven't bitten off more than you can chew. It wouldn't be good for you or Star Gazer."

Jordan wanted to be mad at him for lecturing her, but deep down, she knew he was right. She'd taken on a huge project that she wasn't really equipped to handle. "I know I kind of went about this the wrong way," she admitted. "But I really want to help Star, and I'm willing to work hard and learn."

"Yeah, I guess that's the important part." He placed his hat back on his head. "Did you know the town's already talking about the new city girl who bought the lame draft mare?"

"You're kidding, right?" Jordan was shocked. The national news stations could learn a thing or two about fast reporting from the people in this town.

Jacob grinned. "They think you're crazy for buying a horse that was on its way to the packers. Most of them are betting you won't to be able to pull it off. They think Star will end up right back at the auction within a month."

Jordan crossed her arms and glared at him. "Oh, they do, do they?"

"You can't blame them, Jordan. People around here have been in the livestock business for most of their lives. Gilbert Sutton is a really good horseman, and he chose to get rid of Star because he couldn't deal with her anymore."

Jordan lifted her chin determinedly. "I'll show them," she said. "I'll help Star get better, and then maybe we'll enter that pulling contest against Mr. Sutton. It would serve him right for ditching this mare."

"Take it easy, Jordan." Jacob pulled a couple of carrots out of his pocket. "How about for now, you just concentrate on making Star better? You're going to have your hands full with that."

Jordan picked at the straw bits that clung to her T-shirt. Jacob didn't think she could do it, either. She could tell. And he certainly didn't offer to help her learn anything about riding draft horses or pulling. That stung.

Star Gazer walked over and leaned against the door. She stretched out her neck, asking for a rub. The door creaked under her massive weight and Jordan wondered if the hinges would hold. She was beginning to understand just what Jacob meant about the difference between caring for draft horses and regular horses. She had her work cut out for her.

Jacob handed her the carrots for Star. "Don't worry about it, Jordan. I think you're going to do fine," he said. "I've got a good feeling about this mare. Things are going to work out and you'll both be happy." He gave her an encouraging smile.

Jordan couldn't help but be pleased when he smiled at

her like that. She hoped he was right and that things were going to work out.

"I better get going," Jacob said, hanging Star Gazer's halter on a peg on the wall. "My dad has probably talked your mom's ears off by now. I'll bring that poultice for Star's hooves by in a day or two." He waved good-bye and walked from the barn.

Jordan watched him go, then turned her attention back to Star Gazer. She still couldn't believe the mare was hers. It had really been nice of the Yoders to deliver her. Suddenly she remembered her manners and sprinted up the hill after Jacob. She caught him just as they were about to leave.

"I want to thank you both for all of your help," she said, breathing hard from the uphill run. "I don't know how we would have gotten Star home if you hadn't volunteered to help."

Mrs. McKenzie nodded in agreement. "That's right. Thank you so much for helping my impetuous daughter out of a jam."

Mr. Yoder turned the key in the ignition and the big truck fired up with a rumble. "You're welcome, ladies. It was our pleasure. Helping each other is what it's all about. And don't you worry about that mare, Mrs. McKenzie. I checked her out before I brought her over. She's kind of shy and hangs back in her stall when people are around, but my son says she's taken a real shine to your daughter. She's a mighty big horse, but she's safe. The only thing you have to worry about is minding where your feet are when you're around her."

Jacob laughed. "Yeah, with hooves almost as big as plates, you don't want to get your toe caught under them. Been there and done that. Wasn't much fun."

Jordan grimaced. She couldn't imagine what it would feel like to have a horse that weighed over a ton step on your foot.

She had the feeling that everything about Star Gazer was going to be a learning experience.

They all waved good-bye as the truck pulled out of the driveway. Jordan turned to her mom. "Are you ready to meet the newest member of our family?"

"As ready as I'll ever be."

They walked together to the barn and Jordan opened the stall door to let her mother inside.

Mrs. McKenzie hesitated. "I don't know...she's awfully big," she said. "Maybe I'll just meet her from out here?" She pushed the stall door closed, keeping them both on the outside. "How much hay will a horse this size eat?"

"Jacob said that even though drafts are twice the size of a regular horse, they don't eat twice as much. And they gain weight easily, so I need to be careful that I don't feed her too much."

Star stood at the back of her stall, content to keep her distance. Jordan hoped she'd be able to change the mare's outlook on people. She pulled out one of the carrots Jacob had given her. "Here, Mom, give her this." She held out a carrot of her own, coaxing Star to the door.

Star Gazer caught the scent of the carrot and slowly shuffled forward on tender feet. As she got closer to the door, Jordan's mom backed away.

"Oh, my gosh!" she said, her hand going to her heart. "She's huge! How are you ever going to be able to do anything with her?"

Jordan grinned. "That's the beauty of draft horses," she said, feeding her carrot to the big mare. "There's a reason they call them 'Gentle Giants.' Mr. Yoder says that temperament is bred into them. Now, hold out your carrot in the palm of your hand."

Mrs. McKenzie slowly extended her hand, but as Star

stretched her thick neck to take the treat, Jordan's mom panicked and pulled her hand back.

"Mom!" Jordan laughed. "She's not going to bite you. She just wants the carrot. Now hold your hand out flat so she can take it."

Her mother tried again, but pulled back at the last second. "She's so big it scares me." She chuckled nervously.

"Here, let me show you." Jordan placed her hand under her mother's, holding it steady as Star Gazer reached for the tasty treat.

"Oh my," Mrs. McKenzie said, still hesitating as Star Gazer's big lips moved over the surface of her hand and gently took the carrot. She laughed and wiped the horse slobber off her palm. "That felt so funny. I thought she was going to take my whole hand." She asked Jordan for another carrot.

This was an encouraging sign...and a good first step. Jordan handed her mother another carrot. "This is the last one. We don't want to spoil her too much."

Mrs. McKenzie held the carrot, trying to be brave as Star Gazer stretched her lips to accept the last treat. She only flinched a little bit this time.

"Do you want to pet her?" Jordan asked.

Her mother shook her head and took a step back. "Maybe another day," she said. "I've got to get back up to the house and make us some lunch." At the barn door, she looked back. "Jordan, maybe it's best if you don't get too attached to her? There's a good chance that...that this won't work out. And even if her hooves do get better, you know we can't keep her."

Jordan frowned. *One step forward, two steps back.* She had to come up with a plan to keep Star Gazer.

ten

Four days after Jordan had been put on restriction, her mother lifted the ban. Nicole was even allowed to come back over for visits. Mrs. McKenzie said she was giving her daughter time off for good behavior because she had worked hard and behaved perfectly. But Jordan suspected it might also have something to do with needing help to fix some more of the fence—Nicole had told them she was a great fence builder. Either way, Jordan would be glad to have her friend back. She still had a big list of chores to do; her mother hadn't relented on that.

Jordan immediately called Nicole to give her the good news. She also told her friend the bad news about her mom wanting to find a new home for Star Gazer.

"That's terrible!" Nicole said. "I'll be over as soon as I finish cleaning my room."

An hour later, she met Jordan at the barn. She dismounted and tied Dakota to the hitching post, then followed Jordan into Star Gazer's stall.

"Wow!" Nicole said as she stood beside the draft mare. "I'm tall for a girl, but this still makes me feel really, really small."

Jordan bent down and asked Star to pick up her hoof. The mare hesitated, but then complied with the request. "Look at the size of these feet!" Jordan said as she used the pick to clean the mare's hoof. "You're going to have to help me with these special boots Mr. Yoder dropped off last night. I'm not sure how they work."

Nicole grabbed one of the boots and grinned at Jordan. "Did Jacob come by, too?"

Jordan held the mare's foot steady and made a face at her friend. "No, it was just his father."

"That's too bad." Nicole helped Jordan get the first boot on Star's huge hoof. "Jacob seems pretty shy at school, but I think he's cute. I think he kinda likes you."

Jordan rolled her eyes. "Come on. He's a year older than I am. He likes draft horses and I now own one. He's just being nice to the new girl who doesn't know anything, that's all. He's supposed to come over sometime soon and bring medicine to put on Star's hooves."

"Uh-huh." Nicole waggled her eyebrows.

"It's not like that," Jordan protested. "Really. He's just a nice boy." She slipped the last boot on Star's other hoof, and they stood back to admire their work. "I sure hope these help," Jordan said. "My mom's taking me to the tack store later to buy some hoof oil Jacob and his dad recommended."

Nicole dusted her hands off on her jeans. "Yeah, her feet are really cracked and chipped. They need some serious help. You've got a lot of work ahead of you."

"As soon as Star's feet are better, I'd like to be able to turn her out in that small pasture," Jordan said. "That's less money we'll have to spend on hay and that will make my mom happy. The cheaper it is to feed Star Gazer, the better chance I have of being able to keep her. Do you think you could help me fix the rest of the fence so it will hold Star?"

"Sure," Nicole said. "And if it's too hard for us, my dad can come over and help. He still feels bad that he let you get yourself into this mess."

Jordan unlatched the door and followed Nicole out of the stall. "My mom would probably tell your dad that I'm quite capable of getting into messes all by myself."

She grabbed Star Gazer's halter and lead rope and some pieces of apple. Star Gazer nickered and Jordan smiled. *It's a good feeling when a horse nickers at you,* she thought. *Especially when it's your very own horse.*

Star Gazer lowered her head so Jordan could slip the halter on. "Good girl," Jordan said, holding out a chunk of apple. Star accepted it gratefully and looked for more. "Sorry, girl, you can't have them all at once."

Jordan led the mare out of the stall and snapped her into the crossties in the center of the barn. She grabbed some brushes and a couple of buckets and handed one of the buckets to Nicole.

Nicole laughed. "What am I supposed to do with this?"

Jordan turned her bucket upside down and placed it by Star's head. "I can't even *see* Star Gazer's back from down here, let alone be able to brush it," she said. "Can you?"

"You might have a point there." Nicole turned her bucket upside down and stood on it. "Aha. There it is. I can see it, and it's really, really broad. She looks like a stuffed couch," Nicole hooted.

"Hey, that's my horse you're talking about!"

Jordan ran a comb through Star's mane. She wondered if the mare remembered the times when Karina Sutton had loved and cared for her. "I've got to find a way to convince my mom that we should keep Star Gazer," Jordan said. "She already lost her first family. It wouldn't be fair to her if she just got settled in here and we sold her to someone else."

Jordan paused for a moment. "It's not fun having to leave everything you know and go someplace strange where you have to start all over again."

When Nicole looked over at her, Jordan knew her friend suspected that she wasn't just talking about the horse.

But Nicole didn't ask her about it. "We'll figure something out, Jordan." She tossed her brush into the grooming bucket. "Something will work out. You'll see."

When they finished their grooming session, Jordan led Star back into her stall and they stood back to admire their hand-iwork. "Jacob said people think I'm crazy for buying a lame mare. They think I'm just some dumb city girl who doesn't know what she's doing." She paused for a moment, reaching out to rub Star's cheek. "And maybe I am. But, it would be really neat if we had a chance to prove ourselves. I think I'd like to learn how to drive drafts."

Dakota's whinny sounded outside the barn and Nicole leaned out of the stall to see who he was calling to. "Look at that," she said. "Here comes your knight on a *very* large black horse."

"What?" Jordan turned and peered out the door. Her mouth fell open when she saw Jacob trotting down the hill toward them on a beautiful black Percheron. His horse was so large the ground actually shook when the big hooves hit the terrain. Jacob had a backpack slung over his shoulders. He rode with no saddle; his superb balance kept him right in the middle of his horse.

Star lifted her head, letting out a mighty whinny of greeting. Jacob's horse pulled to a walk and answered the call.

"Hey!" Jacob waved and dismounted, landing with a thud. It was a long way from the horse's back to the ground.

"Wow!" Jordan said. "He's awesome! Can I pet him?"

"Sure." Jacob grinned. "This is my horse, King. I broke him myself. You can ride him if you want."

"Really?" Jordan couldn't believe her luck. Of course she wanted to ride King. She'd never had the opportunity to ride a draft horse before.

"You want to ride too?" Jacob asked Nicole. "He could carry you both at the same time."

Nicole took a small step back. "I've been riding most of my life, but to tell you the truth, King's size kind of scares me a bit. I'll let Jordan handle this one."

"It's okay," Jacob said. "I know these big horses aren't for everyone." He turned to Jordan and cupped his hands for her to put her foot in. "Are you ready to go?"

Jordan stepped forward. Of course she was ready! This would be the next best thing to riding Star Gazer. She reached up to grab a handful of mane to help herself mount, but the Percheron gelding was too tall. "I can't reach his mane." She laughed.

"You'll have to grab it on the way up when I boost you," Jacob said.

Nicole gave them a doubtful look. "I don't know, Jordan. Are you sure you want to do this? There's no saddle, and if you fall off, it's a long way down. Maybe you better ask your mom first?"

"I'll take care of her," Jacob assured. "There won't be any hot-rodding on the first ride."

"At least let me give her my riding helmet," Nicole said, retrieving her hat and handing it to Jordan.

When Jordan had the helmet strapped on, Jacob cupped his hands again and waited for her to mount up. Jordan put her foot into the makeshift stirrup and bounced twice, then held her breath while Jacob boosted her high. She grabbed a handful of mane as she rose into the air and swung her leg over King's broad back.

Jordan straightened up and sat there for a moment, too thrilled even to comment. She felt like she was on top of the world! King shifted his weight and she could feel the muscle power beneath her. It was unlike anything she had experienced on the regular sized horses in L.A.

"Amazing!" she said as she surveyed the area from her perch high atop King's back.

Jacob motioned for Jordan to pick up the reins. "King is plow reined, so you'll have to pull the right rein to go right and the left one to go left."

"Good," Jordan said. "That's just like the English reining I did in my lessons."

"Most drafts also know voice commands," Jacob continued. "If you want to turn right, you say "gee," and if you need to turn left, you say "haw."

"Someday, I'd really like to learn to drive drafts," Jordan said. "Especially now that I have my own. That would be so cool."

Jacob smiled. "I thought driving drafts was just a crazy, spur-of-the-moment thing for you...kind of like buying a lame draft horse at auction," he teased. "But I'm starting to believe that you might really mean it."

Jordan nodded vigorously and Nicole backed her with a thumbs-up.

"Then I guess we better make sure Star gets well." Jacob handed his backpack to Nicole. "I brought some of Brother Fisher's famous cure-all concoction. Some people laugh because they don't believe it works, but they always stop laughing when their horses go sound again. We'll put it on Star's hooves when Jordan's done riding King."

Nicole pulled out the jar and took a sniff. Her face contorted in disgust.

"Sorry," said Jacob. "I should have warned you. But as my dad always says, 'The worse it smells, the better it cures.'"

Jordan peered through the barn at Star, who bobbed her head and nickered to King. "I sure hope it works. I hate to see her limping around. I don't want to think about what might happen if we can't help her."

"Oh, I'm sure it'll help." He looked up at Jordan. "But seriously, you really need to see about getting her x-rayed. All the medicine in the world won't help if she's got a broken bone in those hooves."

Jordan must have involuntarily tightened the reins, because King backed up from the pressure and tossed his head. "Whoa," Jordan said, feeling a bit nervous. She really was a long way off the ground. She forced herself to relax and think positive thoughts. Star was going to be okay. Star was going to be fine.

Jacob turned King so he faced a clear area beside the barn. "When you're ready, just say, 'King, walk up,' and give him a little squeeze with your legs."

Jordan wasn't sure how she was going to give King a leg cue. His back was so wide, her legs were almost sticking straight out. But she did her best and asked the big horse for a walk. King hesitated for a second, like he wasn't sure he understood what she asked, then he stepped forward, placing one massive hoof in front of the other. She could actually feel the ground quiver on each step.

Jordan rocked with the sway of the Percheron's motion, marveling at the strength and size of the horse. It was like sitting on top of a tank, and it was awesome! She asked the big horse for a trot. King responded immediately and she smiled broadly. Surprisingly, his trot was a lot smoother than she expected it to be.

Jacob watched as Jordan trotted King in a big circle around them. "You have really good balance," he said. "Not bad for a *city girl.*" He gave her that same lopsided grin she remembered from the day of the accident.

Jordan ignored the city girl taunt and basked in the compliment about her riding skills. She brought King to a halt and walked him back to where her friends stood. After this experience, she was more determined than ever to help Star get better. It would be so much fun if she could take Star riding with Nicole and her friends from the stable.

Jacob grabbed King's bit and held him still. "Do you want some help getting down?" he asked, but Jordan declined. "It's going to feel like you're falling forever when you dismount," he cautioned her. "Just make sure you land with your knees slightly bent so you don't hurt yourself."

Jordan thought he might be teasing, but when she swung her leg over and pushed off of King's back, it did feel as if she'd dropped from the roof of her house. She landed with a resounding *thump* that jarred every bone in her body and clacked her teeth. Next time, she promised herself, she'd ask for help.

"If you think riding King is fun, you should try driving him," Jacob said, giving his horse a good scratch on the neck.

Nicole took out her phone and snapped a photo of Jordan with Jacob and King. "Is that an invitation?" she asked. "Because Jordan would take you up on it in a heartbeat."

"It would be a dream come true if I could drive Star," Jordan said wistfully.

Jacob studied her for a moment. "I could teach you how to drive if you're really serious," he offered. "School is out and I've got some extra time. It would be fun."

Nicole was standing behind Jacob, and Jordan could see her doing the happy dance and grinning like a fool. She hoped Jacob wouldn't look over his shoulder.

"That'd be really great," Jordan said, trying to keep her voice calm and level when she really wanted to break out in her own version of the happy dance with Nicole. "While I was grounded, I read as much as I could about draft horse care. I even found a website about driving. But I'm sure reading about it isn't the same as getting a personal lesson."

"You've got that right," Jacob said. "A book won't drag you around the field if you get caught up in the driving reins. Or run away with you."

Nicole's eyebrows rose so high they almost disappeared into her hairline. It made Jordan laugh.

"I'm serious," Jacob said. "Working with these big horses isn't for the faint of heart. Even though most of them are very gentle, they're still dangerous just because of their size. They might not mean to hurt you, but if they accidentally step on you or bump you into a fence, it's a lot different than if a regular-size horse does the same thing."

Jordan understood the dangers, but she was willing to take a chance. "I'll do it," she said, extending her hand to shake on the deal. "I'll be a really good student," she promised. Maybe once her mother saw how serious she was about working with Star Gazer, she'd consider letting her keep the mare.

It was worth a try. She'd do anything to give Star Gazer a forever home.

eleven

Jordan held Star Gazer's lead rope while Jacob prepared to pack her feet with the poultice. "Easy, big girl," he said, running his hand gently along Star's thick neck. "I'm just here to help you." He lifted the mare's leg, took off the boot, and motioned for Nicole to hand him the jar.

As soon as Jacob opened it, Jordan and Nicole wrinkled their noses and took a step back.

"Aw, come on, girls. It's not that bad." Jacob said as he scooped a handful of the clay concoction. "First you pack it into the hoof, then press it down along the frog—this part in the middle—and smooth it over the sole." He unfolded a piece of the special paper he'd brought and used it to cover the entire mess. "Okay. Now hand me the boot."

Jacob slipped the boot onto the hoof and moved to the other side of the horse. He repeated the procedure, then stood back to let the horse get used to the poultice.

Star Gazer shifted uneasily in the boots and bent her head to sniff the strange smell. She blew through her nostrils and lifted her upper lip to show the underside in a big horse laugh.

Jordan and Nicole giggled. "See," Jordan said. "Star thinks it's stinky, too."

Star Gazer tugged at her lead rope, wanting to go to her manger to grab a bite of hay. When Jordan didn't comply, the big mare moved anyway, dragging Jordan along with her.

"Hey, wait!" Jordan cried, stumbling along after her horse. "Whoa!"

But Star didn't stop until her head was deep into the feeder and she had pulled out a mouthful of hay.

"Don't let her do that," Jacob said. "If Star gets the idea she can do whatever she wants, she'll be dragging you all over the place."

Jordan held onto the lead rope but her hands were shaking. She'd never had any of the horses at her lessons do that. It felt like her rope had been hooked to the bumper of a moving car and she was being dragged along behind it. She was reminded once again of the raw power of a draft horse.

Nicole looked puzzled. "But how can someone Jordan's size control a horse that big?"

"The same way you control your horse," Jacob said. "You just have to be patient, kind yet firm, and show them who's boss. And you better hope it's not the *horse*," he teased.

Jacob cleaned the clay off his hands, then took the lead rope from Jordan. He tugged on it, asking Star to raise her head, but the mare ignored him. He shouted Star's name in a firm voice and gave a quick tug on the halter, causing the nose band to tighten briefly across the bridge of her nose. He now had her full attention. Star immediately raised her head and followed Jacob back to the center of the stall.

"There." He handed the mare back to Jordan. "Make her mind, or you're going to have a real problem on your hands."

Jordan stared at the big mare, feeling very unsure of herself. "But if I'm mean to her, she won't like me," Jordan said, her voice trembling.

Jacob sighed. "Jordan, you're not some city girl taking a dog down the sidewalk of L.A. That's a two-thousand-pound animal you've got hold of. Making a horse behave is *not* being mean. If you can't be firm and make her obey, you might as well get rid of her right now. A horse this big that thinks she's the boss? She'll eat your lunch." Jacob shook his head as if he was having doubts about working with her.

"I'll do it," Jordan said, tightening her grip on the lead rope and praying that Star wouldn't drag her to the manger again. "I'll learn, Jacob. You'll see."

He studied her for a moment. "Okay, everything's fine. I just want you to understand how serious this is. Star Gazer is not a toy. She's going to take some real work and you need to be up to the challenge."

"I am," Jordan assured him.

"All right, then. That was lesson number one. Make sure you learn it, or there's no sense going any further."

Jordan swallowed hard. She hoped she was up to it.

Jacob handed the jar and the papers to Nicole since Jordan had her hands full. "Leave that clay on there for a couple of days," he advised, "and we'll see if it pulls some of the sting out of those feet. In the meantime, I'm going to see if my friend Daniel Miller will let me use his old mare so we can get you started on lessons. If we can get Star's feet fixed, we'll need to make sure you're at a level to be able to help her in her training."

Jordan took a deep breath and let it out. Jacob was willing to give her another chance. She took off Star's halter before the mare could drag her again and left the stall. "Why can't we use King?" she asked.

Jacob packed his bag and grabbed King's bridle off the hook. "He's a good horse, but he's not the right one for your first lesson. Dan Miller has a really good team of older mares that are perfect for beginners to work with." He tipped his head toward Star Gazer's stall. "You saw what just happened there… Imagine trying to work with a team of fully harnessed horses and a cart when you don't have any control."

Jordan got his meaning, along with the not-so-subtle message that she didn't yet know what she was doing. It hurt her feelings, but it made her determined to try harder. She wanted to prove to Jacob and to Star Gazer that she could handle draft horses.

When Jacob led King out of the barn, Star whinnied at King's departure. Jordan laid a steadying hand on her neck to calm her, then went outside, where she found Jacob mounting up from a fence rail.

"Thanks a bunch for your help," Jordan said. "I'll let you know if Star's feet improve." She waved good-bye, then turned to Nicole. "My mom is taking me to the feed store later. Do you want to go?"

"Sure. I'll put Dakota in the pen behind the barn."

"Okay. I'll meet you up at the house."

While Nicole put her horse away, Jordan slipped back into Star's stall. The mare nickered softly and lipped Jordan's pocket, looking for a treat. She gave her the last carrot tidbit. "I shouldn't be spoiling you like this," she said with a heavy sigh. "You made me look really bad today in front of Jacob."

Star lowered her head and Jordan touched her forehead to hers. "We've got to work together as a team, girl. You remember how to do that, don't you? I'm taking lessons so we'll be able to do fun things together. But you've got to help me out, too." She placed a kiss on the end of Star's nose, then let herself out of the stall.

Nicole caught up with her on the back porch. They did a quick washup in the kitchen sink, then followed Jordan's mom out to the car.

The feed store was a short drive away. They pulled into the parking lot and Jordan immediately recognized the local veterinarian's black truck among the other cars. She hadn't seen Dr. Smith since he helped them with old Ned after the accident. Another truck on the far side of the lot had a big sign painted on its door: Sutton Percherons, Champion Pulling Team Four Years in a Row.

Mrs. McKenzie turned off the motor and lifted her sunglasses to get a better look. "Isn't that the farm Star Gazer came from?"

"Yes," Jordan said as she got out of the car. She frowned at the vehicle. She felt the urge to kick the tires and toss rocks at the shiny red paint job for the way the man had treated Star Gazer.

Seeming to sense her thoughts, Nicole grabbed Jordan by the arm and pulled her along to the door of the feed store.

As they went in, Dr. Smith smiled and waved to them. "Hey, I hear you're the proud new owners of a draft horse." At their surprised look, he replied, "Leroy Yoder told me you picked up one of Gilbert's mares at the auction this past weekend."

Gilbert Sutton laid his purchases down on the counter and turned to see who Dr. Smith was talking to. "You shouldn't have wasted your money," he said to them. "That mare is useless. I once thought she'd be prime breeding stock and a dynamite pulling mare, but she proved me wrong."

Useless? Jordan felt the heat of anger creeping up her cheeks. She wanted nothing more than to scream at Mr. Sutton at the top of her lungs, but she knew she'd be in big trouble if she did. How could the man be so heartless? She wished her father were here to put Sutton in his place. Her dad would have stood up to him. *Or maybe not...* Her dad was pretty good at running away.

Mrs. McKenzie had no problem confronting the arrogant man. "Star Gazer is a lovely horse," she said. "All except for her feet. The poor thing can hardly walk. Tell me, Mr. Sutton, what happened to those feet?"

Jordan's mouth dropped open. Her mother was defending Star Gazer?

Mr. Sutton glared at Jordan's mom. "I didn't do anything to her feet," he said. "The mare wasn't pulling, so she wasn't worth keeping shoes on. Maybe she's stone bruised or something. I didn't *do* anything to her."

"Well, I certainly hope not," Mrs. McKenzie continued. "There are laws against animal cruelty, aren't there?"

Jordan wanted to jump up and cheer for her mom.

A stocky boy sauntered up to the front of the feed store, and Jordan sucked in her breath. It was Tommy Sutton, one of the boys who had caused the accident. She had hoped that he was in juvenile hall someplace, but here he stood, all cocky and self-assured. He locked eyes with Jordan and let out an undignified snort. "That mare's not worth your efforts," he said. "You should have just let the packers have her. If my dad and me couldn't do anything with her, *you* certainly won't be able to. You're wasting your time and money on that cull."

Dr. Smith interrupted the conversation before it got out of hand. "Would you like me to come take a look at that mare for you?"

Jordan's mom smiled her thanks to the vet while giving Gilbert Sutton the hairy eyeball. "Well, thank you, we'd really appreciate that, Dr. Smith. Jordan would like to get some X-rays of Star's hooves, but I told her we'd have to wait until my next paycheck."

"I understand," the vet said. "But I hear Jordan is really good at cutting grass and weeding gardens. Why don't we set up an appointment time now? I'd be happy to take the fee for those X-rays out in trade."

"That would be great!" Jordan breathed a sigh of relief. "Thanks a bunch, Doc. We'll be ready whenever you are."

Gilbert Sutton paid for his feed. "What do you plan on doing with that old mare, anyway?"

Jordan lifted her chin and stared the man right in the eye. "I plan to enter the log-pulling contest at the fair this year. And I'm going to do my best to win it."

Jordan heard snickers around them and Tommy outright guffawed. Mr. Sutton, red-faced, didn't even bother replying to her. He just stuffed his receipt in his pocket and left.

Probably for the better, Jordan thought. *I just issued a challenge I can't possibly live up to.*

Nicole put her arm around Jordan's shoulders. "Don't let Mr. Sutton bother you. He's a mean, nasty man."

"He's mean *and* rude!" Mrs. McKenzie said. "What grown man would taunt a kid like that and make fun of an injured horse? And that boy…," she sputtered. "If he were my child, he'd have so many chores heaped on him, he'd never see the light of day!"

The veterinarian set his purchases on the counter. "Just ignore him. Sutton's pretty full of himself, and his son seems to be following in the same footsteps. If you're going to move in the world of draft horses around this area, you better get used to it, because Sutton Farm *is* draft horses. It's not worth getting yourself worked up about."

Nicole looked at Jordan. "Did you really just tell the four-time log-pulling champion of the county fair that you're going to whup him at this year's event?"

"I believe she did," the cashier said, and everyone chuckled.

Jordan knew they were laughing *with* her, not *at* her. She managed a smile, but she was sure it came out looking rather sickly. She had challenged the man. And she'd meant it. She remembered the advice her mother had given her several years ago when she'd made a rash promise: "Don't write checks you can't cash, honey."

With no horse-driving experience, limited riding skills, and a lame mare that was still at risk of being put down, Jordan had written a very large check. And at the moment, she couldn't possibly cash it.

Jordan heaved a sigh and walked to the vitamin section to find the product she'd come for. She should have kept her mouth shut. When her boastful pronouncement got out around town—and in this place it definitely would—she was going to be the laughingstock of North Adams. She could see the headlines of the local paper now: Stupid City Girl with Lame Horse Challenges Champ.

She hoped Jacob would still speak to her after he heard what an idiot she'd been.

twelve

The next morning, Jordan went down to the barn to feed and groom Star Gazer. The chickens came out to greet her, their hopeful clucks reminding her that they needed feeding, too. The moment she pulled open the heavy barn door, Star nickered and bobbed her head. "I'm coming, girl," she said. "Give me a minute to take care of the chickens and fix your grain."

She scattered some hen scratch in front of the barn and watched the chickens pick the small bits of feed from the grass. Later, she'd gather the eggs they'd laid.

Star whinnied, urging her to hurry with her breakfast. Jordan mixed the vitamins in with the biotin supplement that was supposed to help Star's feet and added a dash of corn oil to make her coat shiny.

"When you get better and you're exercised regularly, I'll up your ration," she told the big black mare. "But until then, you're on a restricted diet."

She opened the stall door and stepped inside. Star Gazer stretched her lips toward the grain can, and Jordan had to dodge her attempts at sneaking a bite out of the can before it was poured into her feed bucket. She knew Jacob would probably scold her for this, but it had become a fun game they played each morning at feeding time. Jordan chuckled and planted a big kiss on the mare's soft, whiskered muzzle.

Jordan couldn't help wondering if Karina Sutton had done the same thing with Star. Did the mare feel better now that there was someone to pay special attention to her again? She sure hoped so. Star Gazer deserved that extra attention no matter what Sutton and his no-good son said.

She wrapped her arms around the mare's thick, muscled neck and breathed in the warm horse scent. Star stretched toward the feed can and tried to get her nose inside.

"Okay, I see where your heart lies." Jordan teased. "Let's get you fed." Star followed her to the feeder and Jordan thought it looked like she was walking a little better. "Want to eat outside today?" she asked, taking the grain can and coaxing the draft mare through the door.

Jordan smiled when she realized it wasn't her imagination. Star Gazer actually took a little bigger stride and seemed to put more weight onto her front hooves. "Yes!" she muttered to herself, and Star's ears flicked back and forth to catch the sound.

Jordan dumped the grain in an outside feeder and went to get the brush bucket and the small stepladder she'd borrowed from the house so she could reach the mare's tall back. She climbed onto the top step of the ladder and rested her hand on Star's withers while she moved the rubber curry in a circular motion over the draft's broad back. She daydreamed about throwing her leg over Star's back and riding her around the pen. It would be so easy.

Star Gazer had been trained to pull loads, but Jordan wasn't sure if she had been broken to ride. Maybe Jacob or his dad could find out for her. She sure didn't plan on asking Mr. Sutton or Tommy.

Jordan leaned some of her weight on Star. The mare lifted her head from the feeder and turned to look at her, then went back to eating. That was a good sign. At least she didn't jet out from under her. She leaned over Star Gazer's back again and was thinking about throwing her leg over when her mother called from the doorway.

"Jordan? Are you in here?" Mrs. McKenzie stepped into the barn and spotted her daughter in the corral portion of Star's living quarters. "Silly question. Of course, you're here. There's a horse in the barn." She walked over to the corral.

"Hi, Mom, what's up?" Jordan climbed down from the step stool and gathered the brushes.

"How's she doing today? Any change in her feet?"

"I think so," Jordan said, "but I don't want to jinx it."

"The vet called. He said he's going to stop by tomorrow morning to do the X-rays," her mother said.

"Excellent!" Jordan smiled, but a piece of her was afraid to find out the results. What if the news was bad? *Really bad?* She put on a brave face for her mother. "It will be good to know for sure what the problem is."

Her mother entered the pen, still looking a little apprehensive, but she came to stand next to Jordan and Star. She pulled an apple from her pocket and offered it to the big mare.

Star Gazer stretched her neck and took the apple in one big bite, rolling the juicy fruit around in her mouth so she could get it between her teeth and crunch it.

"That wasn't very ladylike." Jordan's mom admonished the big mare. "I should have cut it into pieces." She reached out her hand and gave Star Gazer a nervous pat.

Star swallowed the apple, then dropped her head to the grain bucket.

"You had another phone call a few minutes ago…" Jordan's mom gave her a conspiratorial smile. "It was Jacob. He asked me for permission to give you horse-driving lessons. He said Daniel Miller has agreed to let you use his team at their farm, and I'm supposed to drive you over there at noon if you're interested. He even offered to teach me, too, but I think for now, I'll just watch. Are you going to take him up on the offer?"

Jordan bobbed her head enthusiastically. "It's going to be so much fun. I can't wait! Are you sure you don't want to learn, too, Mom?" She crossed the corral and let herself out of the stall, then tossed Star a flake of hay. "Someday we might be able to drive Star in a cart. I think you'd like that."

Her mother looked at her with a sad smile. "Jordan, you know we can't keep this horse," she said. "I'm really glad you're enjoying this experience, but we can't keep Star." She reached out and brushed a lock of Jordan's hair behind her ears. "Look at the bright side, though. You've made some nice friends in Nicole and Jacob, and probably this Daniel, too. They've all got horses and I'm sure they'll let you come ride them anytime you want."

Jordan busied herself with straightening the hay pile. She didn't want her mother to see the tears in her eyes.

"I spoke to Mrs. Miller after Jacob called," her mom continued. "She said her husband will be there supervising you kids, and he assured me there's nothing to worry about. I'm going to drop you off, then go to the store and do some stocking while you're taking your lesson."

"Sounds like a plan," Jordan said, keeping her head down.

Her mom brushed some bits of hay off the front of her shirt. "You finish here and I'll go up to the house and make us an early lunch." She turned to leave, then looked back at

Star Gazer. "Do you really think Star could beat Sutton in that pulling contest if her feet got better?"

Jordan shrugged. "I don't know," she answered. "But Jacob said she used to be one of Sutton Farm's top pulling mares. They had big plans for her before something went wrong."

Jordan's mom nodded and walked away, leaving Jordan to wonder what all that was about. She grabbed the wheelbarrow and a pitchfork and pushed them to Star's stall. Soon, she'd get to trade in her cleaning tools for driving reins. She couldn't wait!

* * *

A few hours later, they pulled into the Millers' place. Jordan had always enjoyed looking at it whenever they drove by, but it was even prettier up close.

Like many of the farmhouses in this area, the Millers' two-story brick house was almost a hundred years old and very well kept. The lawns were perfectly manicured, and colorful mums and marigolds overflowed the flower beds. The big red barns and stable yard were immaculate. Horse-drawn farm implements and carriages were parked nearby. In the green pastures beyond the barns, at least a dozen golden Belgian draft horses grazed in the fields. To Jordan, this place was paradise.

Jacob came out of the barn with an armload of harness collars. His hands were too full to wave, but he tipped his head in their direction when he spotted them. Jordan could see Daniel and his dad leading a team of Belgians from the side pasture.

Suddenly, Jordan got a bad case of nerves. She'd been waiting for this moment, but now that it was here, she didn't want to get out of the car. What if she messed up and made a fool of herself? She'd already done that several times since they'd moved here. What if she made a mistake and did something that hurt the horses? Or what if they were just too big and strong for her and she couldn't physically do it?

"Everything okay?" her mom asked.

"Yeah, I guess, "said Jordan. "I'm just feeling kind of out of place. Everyone here is a real pro at driving drafts and I'm going to feel really stupid."

Her mother reached over and squeezed her hand. "Everyone has to start somewhere, sweetheart. We can't all be professionals at everything. Just do your best and enjoy learning something new. I'm sure Jacob would never make fun of you."

Jordan smiled at her mother and stepped out of the car. "Thanks, Mom." She hoped her mother was right. Jacob and Daniel had been driving draft horses for years. Surely they wouldn't make fun of her when she tried to join their ranks.

There was only one way to find out...

Putting one foot in front of the other, Jordan marched toward the barn where the horses were waiting.

thirteen

"Hi, Jordan, glad you could make it," Jacob said as he waved her over. "Let me introduce you to everyone." He clapped the farm owner on the back. "This is Mr. Miller. And over there is my best friend, Daniel."

The Miller boy peeked out from behind a large mare he'd just tied to the post. "Hi, Jacob tells me you were the one who rescued him and Brother Fisher in the buggy accident."

Jordan just smiled. She felt kind of overwhelmed with so many talented horse people around.

Jacob set down the harness collars. "Hopefully, we won't have any buggy accidents here." He looked directly at Jordan and smirked.

Mr. Miller tied the other horse next to the one tethered to the post and grabbed a set of brushes to groom them. He gave Jordan a wink. "Don't let these boys give you a bad time, missy. If I'm not mistaken, one of them took out a fence post last week when they were practicing."

Daniel shoved his hands into his jeans pockets and kicked at the dirt.

Jordan looked up in surprise. "Really?"

The boy shrugged. "The post was rotten. It needed replacing anyway."

Everyone shared in the laugh.

Mr. Miller pointed toward the house where a middle-aged woman and a teenage girl were sitting on the porch. "That's my wife and daughter up there," he said. "They're working on some stitching right now. You'll get to meet them later." He squinted and looked across the field. "Daniel's got a younger brother and sister hiding around here someplace. I'm sure you'll meet them, too. But for now, let me say that we're happy to have a fresh face in town. And it's really nice to see a young lady interested in draft horses. A lot of the girls around here ride them fancy show horses." He laughed. "They're more like lap dogs than horses."

Jordan thought he must be talking about Nicole's riding friends from the stable.

Jacob took a brush and started grooming one of the Belgians. "Now, let me introduce you to the horses. This here's Candy," he said. "She's the right-hand mare. The other one is Suzie. She pulls on the left. They're full sisters, a year apart. Normally, we hook them together and drive them as a team—which you'll do later on after you've mastered one horse. But today, we're going to harness them separately, and you'll take one horse while Dan takes the other," he said. "I'll walk beside you to make sure you don't get into trouble."

"Like getting dragged around the barnyard?" Jordan asked.

"Yeah, something like that," Jacob grinned.

Mr. Miller handed Jordan a brush. "You're here to learn, so you might as well jump right in." He stood back so she could get to work. "I hear you bought one of Gilbert Sutton's mares."

"Yes, I bought her at the auction," Jordan said as she ran the brush over the golden coat, marveling at how beautiful the two huge draft horses were.

"If I remember right, that was quite a pulling mare," Mr. Miller said. "Gilbert won several competitions with her. Then one day, they say she just quit pulling. I hear he tried her several times; he even gave her to his son Tommy for a while. That kid ruined the mare as far as I'm concerned. Sutton got so darned mad when Star Gazer wouldn't cooperate that he gave up on her and turned her out to pasture."

Jordan kept brushing. The story made her feel sad and angry. Mr. Sutton shouldn't have stopped loving Star just because things didn't go his way.

"Hey, you missed a spot," Jacob said, bringing Jordan back to the present.

She looked up at him, glad that he had broken into her thoughts. She wasn't going to let anything spoil this special day. She was with friends and working with horses. Everything she learned here would help her with Star.

Mr. Miller handed her a hoof pick and helped her get the first foot lifted off the ground. "That mare of yours has great bloodlines, but Gilbert didn't even want to breed her. Said he didn't want to pass on the lazy gene. Truth be told, I think the mare just sulked on him. She really loved Sutton's daughter. I think that mare gave up once the girl left for college." He helped her pick up the draft's other large foot. "But that's just my opinion."

Jordan took in all of the information. She'd do whatever it took to help Star Gazer become a good skidding horse again. From what everyone had told her, it seemed that Star had once loved it.

Jacob pulled out a small bench and placed it beside the horse Jordan was brushing so she could stand on it to reach its back and the crest of its neck. When they were done with the grooming, they moved the horses to the harnessing area. Jordan was fascinated with the setup.

The harnessing station looked similar to the decking that went around the outside of an above-ground swimming pool. It stood about four feet off the ground and had three sides to it, like a squared-off horseshoe.

"What's this for?" Jordan asked.

"We use it for harnessing the horses. They can be led in and tied in the center."

"How does it work?"

While the boys moved the horses into the station and tied them to the rings on the railing, Mr. Miller explained. "Harness is heavy," he said. "Especially if it's heavily spotted. It's easier to drop it down on their backs from this platform than it is to throw it up on their tall backs from the ground."

"I see," Jordan said. "But what do you mean by 'heavily spotted'?"

"Spotting is the big silver dots they put on harness for decoration," Daniel explained. "Work harness for the fields usually doesn't have any spotting, but show harness is loaded with it. People who show their horses want the harness to be flashy. It makes the harness heavier, though."

"Oh, and just so you know," Jacob said, "Mr. Fisher and the people in his Amish community don't use spotted harness. They believe it's prideful and not necessary."

Jordan smiled to herself . Simple harness would go along with the Amish people's simple lifestyle. She was beginning to understand some of the differences between the Amish community and the Mennonites.

Mr. Miller handed Jacob and Daniel bridles. "We'll let the boys put on the bridles and harness collars today, Jordan. You can stand by and watch this part. But we'll let you help with the harnessing."

Jordan felt a shiver of excitement. She was actually learning how to harness a draft horse! Someday soon she might get to harness Star Gazer. She wasn't sure how or where she was going to get her own equipment—it was pretty expensive.

"Now comes the difficult part," Mr. Miller said. "We're going to put the rest of the harness on these horses and attach it to the collars so we have one complete pulling unit."

Jacob bumped Jordan with an elbow. "I'll help if you don't think you can do it. This harness probably weighs about half of what you do."

Jordan bristled. Was he saying she was a helpless girl? "I can do it," she said.

"You're going to get your chance right now," Mr. Miller said. "You'll learn to appreciate this raised decking. It cuts your workload and makes it possible for someone your size to harness a big horse."

"Come on, then, Jordan," Jacob said. "Dan and I will take you to the harness room and show you how it's done."

As she followed them, Jordan noticed the knowing looks that passed between the guys. She could tell they weren't sure she could handle this, but she was determined to prove them wrong. She'd seen harness before—just not close-up and in person. Like everyone, she'd seen the famous Budweiser Clydesdales on the TV commercials. Harness was just a bunch of pieces of leather stitched together. How heavy could it be—even with the silver spots on it?

They stepped into the harness room and Jordan felt her jaw drop. She stared for a moment, then breathed deeply, taking in the wonderful scent of well-oiled leather. All around them, on big hooks and harness racks, hung driving reins, harness collars, and work harness. Against the wall, in oak display cases with glass fronts, was heavily spotted, prized show harness. She'd seen pictures of it in magazines and in those famous commercials with the Clydesdales. It was even more impressive than she'd imagined.

"Here's the one you'll be using." Jacob pointed to a work harness on a long rack. "We lay our harness out from front to back to keep it in order. Those long metal pieces at the front of it are what we call the 'hames.' They go on the collar and connect the whole thing together."

Jacob showed Jordan how to position herself. "You need to start at the front, like this, take a hame in each hand and run your arms all the way up through the center of it. This will keep it all in order when you pick it up. That makes it easier when you transfer it from here to where the horses are and place it on Candy's back."

Jordan thought it sounded simple enough, but she didn't like the way Jacob was looking at her—like he knew something she didn't. She watched Daniel grab Suzie's harness. At first it looked easy, but then she noticed the way his muscles strained when he pulled the harness from the rack. She was beginning to understand why the boys had given each other that knowing glance. This was going to be tougher than she thought.

"Okay, let's go," Jacob said. "I'll help if you need it."

Jordan gave an unladylike snort. If she was forced to the ground from the weight of the harness, she *might* ask Jacob for help. But her pride and her stubborn streak would make that a last resort.

She took a hame in each hand and ran her arms up through the harness. She could barely fit it all on, so she tipped her arms up to make sure the harness wouldn't slip off and drop to the ground. Taking a deep breath, she pulled upward and away from the rack. When the full weight of the harness hit her, she took another big breath and tried to balance herself.

The harness was heavy and awkward to hold. She wasn't

quite sure how she was going to carry it to where the horses were waiting, but she was determined to try. Putting one foot in front of the other, she followed Daniel out the door. Jacob trailed behind her, waiting to take over if she requested it. *Not gonna happen!* she thought as she gritted her teeth and marched on.

She wasn't exactly sure how she made it up the four steps to the platform without tipping over, but she smiled triumphantly when she reached Candy's side. Now she understood why Mr. Miller had built the platform. There was no way she could toss this harness up onto a draft horse's back—especially after carrying it that far.

Jacob guided her into position beside Candy. "Let me show you how we do this part." He put his arms under hers and showed her how to place the hames up high on the withers so they could be attached to the collar.

Jordan felt her face flush at the feel of Jacob's arms guiding hers. Her brain went in a couple of different directions and she missed some of the things he was saying. But together they laid the harness out along the horse's back with the padded loop Jacob called the crupper going under the tail, and the thick breech strap across the wide part of the horse's hindquarters.

"There, you did it," Jacob said. "Good job!"

Everyone agreed and Jordan felt her spirits soar. She could do this!

Mr. Miller showed her how to hook up the different straps so everything would stay in place and secure. Finally, they attached the long driving reins to the bridle and ran them through the rings on the harness. They were ready to drive.

The sense of accomplishment Jordan felt when she looked at the harnessed mares surprised her. Working with horses and learning new things was fun. This could turn out to be a great summer!

"Should we go into the front paddock," Jacob asked, "or the big field?"

Mr. Miller backed Candy out of the harnessing station and headed her to the front paddock. "We'll start in the small enclosed area until I'm sure Jordan's able to control this horse. We'll save the big field for when we start her on the cart...just so she doesn't run into anything."

When the boys all laughed, Mr. Miller turned to Jordan. "Those boys wouldn't be hee-hawing like that if I showed you the video of *them* learning how to drive a horse and carriage."

"Oh, yeah?" Jordan ran ahead to open the paddock gate, then hurried back to hear the story.

"You'd better believe it," Mr. Miller said. "Daniel here took out my hitching post and a cart tire by cutting a turn too short. And Jacob there wiped out the side of his dad's old horse trailer."

Even though Daniel and Jacob weren't laughing anymore, that news didn't make Jordan feel much better. If two boys who had been raised around draft horses could make such big mistakes, what chance did *she* have? She'd die of embarrassment if she took out a stretch of fencing or hit the side of the barn.

Daniel and his dad drove the horses through the gate and stopped them in the center of the large dirt paddock. "Step on over here, Jordan," Mr. Miller said, offering her the driving reins.

Jordan stood there for a moment, frozen like the big horse statue at the head of the Miller's driveway.

"Come on, Jordie," Jacob encouraged her. He took the reins from Mr. Miller and motioned her forward. "I'll be right here with you. I won't let anything happen to you."

Jordie? Her grandmother was the only one who had ever called her that, and it was a long time ago. But Jordan liked the way it sounded when Jacob said it. Her legs felt a little wobbly when she stepped forward to take the reins, mostly because of nerves, but partly because of the boy's warm smile. Nicole would give her a good-natured poke and say she was smitten. But Jordan told herself that she just liked hanging around Jacob because he was smart and nice.

To be safe, Jacob and Mr. Miller positioned her several feet behind the horse, just out of kicking range. Jordan was surprised to see that the correct hold for the driving reins was pretty much the same as the one she'd learned in her English riding lessons, but these reins were wider, and there were many feet of reins left over. Mr. Miller showed her how to fold the remaining reins and toss them over her shoulder so she wouldn't get caught in them.

Jordan stood behind the big cream-colored hindquarters of the Belgian mare, unable to see anything directly in front of her but the horse. The wide reins felt unfamiliar in her hands, and she couldn't get comfortable with the length of rein hanging over her shoulder.

She waited—half excited, half terrified—for the instructions that would teach her how to drive and work as one with the giant Belgian mare, and eventually with Star. This was the moment she'd been waiting for.

fourteen

Relax, Jordan," Jacob said. "You're surrounded by four fences. Even if something crazy happens—which it won't—you can't go very far. There are three of us in here to help you, okay? Dan will be driving Suzie beside you to keep your horse going in a straight line, and we'll be right here to help. You're going to do fine."

Jordan glanced over at Dan. He gave her a shy but encouraging smile.

Jacob readjusted Jordan's hand position on the reins. "This will actually be easier than your English riding lessons because you won't have to worry about cueing the horse with your legs. The turns are exactly the same; you just add a voice command to each horse you're driving. When you want to walk or trot, you call the horse by its name, ask them for the gait, and add a chirp to the cue."

Mr. Miller interrupted him before he could finish. "Just remember not to act like they do in the old Western movies and start flapping those reins on the horse's rump."

Jordan frowned in confusion. That was exactly what she'd planned to do—shake the reins along with a cluck and the voice command to walk.

"You don't want to get used to slapping them with the reins to make them go forward," Mr. Miller said. "Sometimes you need to lower your reins so you can stop and rest. If a horse gets used to moving forward as soon as he feels the reins dropping on his back, you could be in a lot of trouble. When you want to just stop and stand for a while, he'll think you're asking him to go fast."

Jordan understood. She certainly didn't want a runaway. Even at a slow pace, these big horses were intimidating enough.

"So when you want to turn right, say the horse's name, then 'come around, gee,'" Jacob instructed. "If it's left, then call out, 'Candy, come around, haw.'"

Jordan completed the list. "And for stopping I'll say, 'Candy, whoa,' with little tugs on the bit. Right?"

"Looks like you're ready to go," Daniel said. "You've got your turns and your brakes figured out. Let's get started."

Jordan's hands were shaking and it was hard to keep a tight grasp on the reins. Candy started to fuss, pulling at the bit to ease the pressure. Jordan took a steadying breath and tried to calm down. She *had* to do this correctly.

"Think about what you want to do," Jacob instructed. "Visualize what you want and make it happen."

Jordan closed her eyes for a second, then said, "Candy, walk up," following the command with a loud clucking of her tongue.

The mare stepped forward at a brisk walk. And even though Jordan had given the command, she still wasn't prepared for the tug on the reins as it pulled her along in the horse's wake, her arms outstretched as she tried to regain her balance and footing.

"Take bigger steps," Jacob said as he walked behind her, trying to keep her safe and correct her cues.

Jordan did as he asked but it took another thirty feet of traveling before she was able to match her walking speed to Candy's and get the proper amount of contact with the horse's bit. She had a hard time keeping the extra length of rein balanced on her shoulder and it ended up unraveling and trailing behind her. But the hardest adjustment was not being able to see what was directly in front of the horse. Jordan could see things on each side of Candy, but walking behind the tall, wide mare blocked her view of what lay ahead.

They came to the fence line and Jordan had to decide if they were going right or left. Since Daniel drove his horse to the left of them, Jordan decided to turn right. Her brain went into a spin as she tried to remember the voice command for a right turn.

"Candy, gee!" she said at the last moment, and the big mare turned to the right. Jordan grinned broadly. She'd done it! She was in command and working as one with the big Belgian mare—for the moment.

They worked for another thirty minutes, practicing turns and backing up until the cues were firmly planted in her mind. Finally, Mr. Miller called it a day. He held the gate open while they drove the horses through and back to the harnessing area. Jordan found it much easier to take the harness off the horse than it had been to put it on. Still, she was relieved when Mr. Miller brought her a wheelbarrow to take the harness back to the tack room.

"You did really well today, Jordan," Mr. Miller said. "One more session like this and I think we can get you started in the cart."

"That would be great!" Jordan said. "Thank you!"

She couldn't wait to tell her mom and Nicole about her lesson. She'd had so much fun driving Candy she couldn't even imagine how awesome it would be to drive Star Gazer. Tomorrow, the vet would be out to take X-rays. Then they'd know exactly what they were dealing with. Jordan wondered if she'd ever be able to hook Star to a cart—or maybe someday, to a set of big logs in a pulling contest.

* * *

The following morning, Jordan let out the lead rope and Star Gazer lowered her head to crop the grass in front of the barn. The mare moved much better today; she still stepped tenderly, but she was putting more weight on her feet than normal. It appeared the stinky poultice was working.

The veterinarian would be there soon to take the X-rays. Jordan needed to get the clay washed out of Star Gazer's hooves so the vet could get a clean picture.

She bent to remove the boots, loving the steady *chomp-chomp* as Star cropped grass and the clucking of the speckled hens in the background. She smiled. These sounds were certainly a lot more comforting than the blare of car horns or jets flying overhead! She didn't miss that one bit.

Jordan took off the left boot and picked most of the clay out with a hoof pick. She rinsed the rest of the clay off with the hose and did the other side.

Just as she finished, Jordan heard the muffled sound of hoof beats and the noise of chattering voices. She looked up to see Nicole and a couple of girls on horses coming down the hill.

Star lifted her head and whinnied a greeting, then started walking toward their visitors.

"Whoa!" Jordan said, but it was several steps before the mare stopped. *Like being pulled along like a toy on the end of a string,* Jordan thought. She really was at the mercy of this horse that outweighed her by a ton. She needed to be firm like Jacob had showed her. If Star decided she was going to take off and go, there'd be no stopping her.

Jordan waved as everyone pulled their mounts to a stop. She admired the two fine-boned horses the other girls rode.

"Hi, Jordan," Nicole said. "I brought some of my friends over to meet you and Star."

"Hey, Jordan," the girl with the dark hair said, side-passing her tall bay gelding to a spot of shade. "I'm Kathy and this is Mary." She pointed to the blonde girl beside her. "Nicole's been telling us about you and your new horse. I thought we should come by and greet the new kid in town. We're on our way to the lake if you want to come with us."

Jordan held firm on the lead rope, trying to prevent Star from walking forward to touch noses with the other horses. "Thanks. That sounds like a lot of fun, but we're waiting for the vet to come x-ray Star's feet."

"What's wrong?" Mary asked.

"We aren't sure," Jordan answered. "Some people say it could be a broken bone in the foot or really bad stone bruising. That's the one I'm hoping for."

Kathy moved her horse a little closer. "Wow, Star is huge!" she said. "My horse is almost seventeen hands, and I thought he was big." She wrinkled her nose. "What are you going to do with her? She's too big and clunky to show."

Jordan cringed inside, but she tried not to show her irritation. "Oh, they show draft horses all the time," she said. "Star Gazer won several pulling contests around here when she was younger. And it's a lot of fun to ride a draft horse." She wasn't exaggerating. King had been way more fun to ride than the horses she'd worked with in L.A. "I'll be riding Star

Gazer as soon as we figure out what's wrong with her feet and get her fixed up."

"Wait a minute…you knew she was lame when you bought her?" Kathy asked, her eyebrows rising in disbelief.

Jordan didn't feel like explaining. "Yes, and I'm glad I have her."

Nicole broke in before Kathy could say anything else. "Hopefully, everything will be fine, and maybe in a couple weeks, you can go on rides with us."

Jordan had waited a long time to have her own horse. If she started riding with these girls and got to know some other kids, it might make things easier at school in the fall. "That would be great!" she said.

Kathy scrutinized Star Gazer. "I still don't get it. Why buy a draft horse?" she asked.

"I *like* draft horses," Jordan said, wondering why she had to explain her decision to this girl. Maybe getting into a riding group wouldn't be as much fun as it sounded. Her "big clunky" horse obviously wouldn't fit into Kathy's perfect horse club.

Kathy seemed not to hear Jordan's answer. "Nicole said this is your first horse," she babbled on. "If you'd bought a Quarter horse or a Thoroughbred, you could have entered the shows with us. There's no way a huge, clumsy horse like that could compete with a horse like mine. He's a Dutch Warmblood, you know."

Jordan wanted to tell Kathy that her expensive Warmblood wouldn't be here today if it hadn't been for people crossing drafts with regular horses a long time ago. She looked over at Nicole, wondering what her friend thought of the situation.

Nicole frowned at Kathy. "I like Star, too. I think Jordan will do just fine with her."

Kathy readjusted her feet in the stirrups. "Yeah, I suppose." She turned her horse, preparing to leave, then looked back over her shoulder. "Was that you I saw out at the Miller place yesterday, driving horses with those Amish boys?"

"They're Mennonites," Jordan corrected her. "And yes, that was me. I had a great time there learning to drive draft horses."

Kathy snickered. "Amish, Mennonite...what's the difference? They all dress funny."

Jordan opened her mouth to tell Kathy there was actually quite a bit of difference between the two, but she knew it would be a waste of time. "They're very good horsemen and I learned a lot," she said. "I'm going there again tomorrow."

"Whatever," Kathy said. "See you around." She pointed her Warmblood up the hill and walked off.

Mary smiled at Jordan, then trotted after Kathy, motioning for Nicole to join them.

Jordan glanced at Nicole, feeling a little betrayed.

Nicole lifted Dakota's head with the reins. "I'm sorry, Jordan. Kathy is usually a lot of fun to hang with, but sometimes she can be a big pain. Don't worry about what she thinks. You don't have to ride a horse that looks like hers."

"No problem." Jordan gave her a wave. "Have a good time at the lake and swim a few extra laps for me."

"Yeah, right. Sometimes we don't even get in the water," Nicole said. "Kathy doesn't like to get her hair wet. I'll call you tonight to see what the vet has to say. I hope it's good news."

"Me too," Jordan said. "Talk to you later." She watched her friend ride off with the other girls, feeling a small spike of envy. Going to the lake would have been fun. Hopefully, someday soon, she'd be able to take Star on a ride with them.

She busied herself with brushing Star while the mare

cropped the sweet grass. A few minutes later, the vet pulled into the driveway. Dr. Smith and his assistant stepped out of the truck and unloaded their equipment.

Jordan's mom helped carry the items down to the barn and run the extension cords so they could power the portable X-ray machine.

"Well, let me have a look here," Dr. Smith said as he picked up Star's right front leg. He examined the hoof from several different angles and shook his head. "They certainly didn't leave her much to walk on." He set that hoof down and picked up the other one.

Finally, the vet straightened and wiped his hands on a towel he carried in his back pocket. "It looks like they pulled the shoes off when they weren't using her and let her stand around, probably in a rocky area. Her hooves were brittle and they just chipped off until they were down to the white line. That would be like cutting your fingernails back to the quick, then asking you to put pressure on them."

Jordan winced at the thought. No wonder poor Star limped when she took a step. "What can be done to fix her?"

"That'll depend on what the X-rays show," Dr. Smith said. "For now, keep that poultice and boots on her and continue feeding her those good supplements. If the X-rays are clean, it'll just be a matter of waiting a couple of weeks until her hooves are long enough to be able to tack some shoes on her."

Jordan ran her hand down Star's long beautiful face. "And if the X-rays are bad?"

The vet gave her arm a comforting squeeze. "We'll worry about that when we come to it, kiddo. Now, let's get this done." He motioned for his assistant to set up the machine.

"How long will it take to get the results back?" Jordan's mom asked.

114

Dr. Smith handed the film trays to his assistant along with some lead-lined rubber gloves to limit her exposure to the X-rays. "I'll drop the film at the lab to develop as soon as I leave here. We should know in a couple of hours."

Jordan crossed her fingers. Very soon they would know Star Gazer's fate. But at the moment, two hours seemed like an eternity.

fifteen

Jordan jumped when the phone rang. She'd been sitting on the couch for the last thirty minutes, waiting for the vet to call. She let it ring one more time, then picked up the receiver. "Hello?"

"Hi, Jordan, this is Dr. Smith. I have the results."

Jordan's heartbeat echoed in her ears, making it difficult to hear his voice. She held her breath.

"I have good news and bad," the doctor said. "The good news is, I don't see any chipped or broken bones, or any sign of deterioration in the hoof."

Jordan's breath came out in one big *whoosh*. She knew those were all problems that might have meant a death sentence for Star. She held the phone in the air for a second while she did her little happy dance, then remembered that there was also bad news. She immediately sobered and sat back down on the couch. "What's the bad news, Dr. Smith?"

"Well, it's not going to be clear sailing," the veterinarian warned. "She's got serious problems with her front feet. There's some really deep bruising there, along with a thin sole. And it looks like Star has an abscess in her right front hoof. You need to keep those boots on so there's no more erosion of that hoof wall. I'll be out in a couple of hours to drain that abscess and show you how to take care of it."

"Will she eventually be okay?" Jordan asked.

"It's going to take a while to get those feet back in shape, but if we keep on top of things, there's a good chance Star Gazer will go back to normal. But if she suffers any more trauma to those already damaged hooves, it could run the chance of ruining her for life."

Jordan swallowed hard. She certainly didn't want that. Even though this was the best possible outcome she could have hoped for under the circumstances, there was still a lot of work to be done, and no room for missteps. She could hear the vet shuffling through some papers. She shifted the phone to her other ear while she waited.

"I'm going to give you the number of a farrier who'll come out and clean up the jagged edges on those hooves," Dr. Smith said. "Then in a couple weeks, when her hooves are long enough, you'll need to get some shoes tacked on those feet to keep them protected and encourage growth. If everything goes well, I'd say in four or five weeks she'll be able to start back with light work."

Jordan smiled. Four or five weeks wasn't really that long to wait. It was nothing compared to what she could have been dealing with. She wrote down the phone number of the shoer. "Thanks a bunch, Dr. Smith. I'll do my very best to take good care of Star."

"You're welcome, Jordan. I know you will. Call me anytime you have a question," he said. "Oh, and Jordan...my wife has several flower beds that need some serious weeding. If you take care of those and provide the lawn with a good mowing, we'll call it even on the X-rays."

"That would be great," Jordan said. "As soon as I check with my mother, I'll call Mrs. Smith and make the arrangements." She hung up the phone and took a deep breath.

Her mom walked into the room. "Good news?"

"Yes," Jordan said. "And a little bad news, too, but it's nothing we can't handle. Star has an abscess in one of her feet. Dr. Smith is coming over this afternoon to drain it."

Jordan's mom gave her a quick hug. "I'm so glad," she said. "I was really hoping the news wouldn't be too bad. Star is a sweet mare and deserves better. Hopefully, now that we know there's a chance for recovery, we'll be able to find her a nice family that will take good care of her."

Jordan scrunched up her lips. "*We're* a good family, Mom. Why can't *we* take care of Star?"

Mrs. McKenzie gave an exasperated sigh. "We've been over this, Jordan. I told you the day you bought Star that we wouldn't be able to keep her." She opened the refrigerator and gathered items to make sandwiches. "My job doesn't pay much, and you'll be back in school soon."

"But, Mom," Jordan argued as she placed the plates and silverware on the kitchen table. "I've picked up a lot of good jobs, and I can buy hay with the money I earn. And we've got plenty of pasture. Once Star's feet are better, we could turn her out and we wouldn't need to buy any hay—except in the winter."

Her mother put the mayo and mustard on the table and reached for the milk. "That's part of the problem, Jordan," she said. "We're not in Los Angeles anymore. Michigan has a *real* winter. We're going to have snow and ice. All of those weeding and lawn-mowing jobs won't be here in the winter."

"Oh, yeah." Jordan's face fell. "Maybe I could baby-sit?" she said hopefully.

Mrs. McKenzie placed the bread and sandwich meat on the table along with a plate of lettuce and sliced tomatoes and sat down. "Maybe in a couple of years when we get on our feet, honey."

Jordan looked at the lunch fixings, but she had no appetite. She made herself half a sandwich so her mom wouldn't protest. "It's just that we have Star *now* and she's the horse I want. Why get rid of her and start all over again in a year or two?" She picked at her sandwich. "At first I wasn't so sure about owning a draft horse, but after I got to know Star I can't imagine having any other horse. I love her, Mom. Star needs someone special. All of her people are gone, and the ones she trusted gave her away. Are we going to do the same thing?"

Her mother didn't answer. Jordan knew there wasn't any good answer.

"What time are you supposed to be at the Miller farm today?" Mrs. McKenzie asked, changing the subject.

"Jacob said to be there at one. He said there's going to be a special surprise."

Her mother looked at the clock on the wall. "Then we better hurry. Do you mind if I stay and watch for a little bit today?"

Jordan thought for a moment. "I don't know. I make a lot of mistakes."

When Jordan still didn't say okay, a look of understanding came over her mother's face. "Oh, I get it...you don't want me to *witness* your mistakes?"

Jordan looked down at her plate. "Something like that, yeah."

"Well, whenever you're ready to have me watch, I'll be there." She reached out and patted Jordan's hand. "Just remember...there's no shame in making mistakes. The important thing is that you're out there trying. And you're doing something that makes you happy. Now, eat your sandwich and let's get over there. Jacob and Daniel are waiting.

I'll come home and deal with the vet and Star's abscess while you're having your lesson."

"Thanks, Mom. Don't forget to give Star some carrots. She likes it when you give her treats." *And the more time you spend with Star,* Jordan thought, *the more chance you'll get attached to her.*

She finished her sandwich and put the plate in the sink. "Do you think they're strange?" she asked, leaning against the counter. "The boys, I mean. Do you think they're dweebs because they dress funny and have old-fashioned ways?"

Jordan's mom rose from the table and set her dishes on the counter. "Where did that come from, honey?" She pulled a container of cookies from the cabinet. "We were just talking about Star. How'd we get to boys?"

Jordan shrugged. "I don't know. Nicole finally brought over two of the girls she rides with and one of them was making fun of Jacob and Daniel."

"I don't know anything about that girl, but I know those boys have been awfully nice to you. I know they volunteered to help when they didn't have to. And they're just about the most well-mannered teenagers I've ever run across." She grabbed the car keys off the hook by the light switch. "Yes, they might dress a bit different, but hey, look at half the kids your age… Do you really think *they* dress normal?"

Jordan laughed. "You might have a point there."

Her mother handed her a chocolate chip cookie. "I'm happy you're making some nice friends here," she said. "Now grab your stuff and let's go."

* * *

As soon as they arrived at the Miller farm, Jordan bolted out of the car, ready to get started. She still felt a little intimidated about making mistakes in front of everyone, but she was excited to be learning so much. And who could complain about getting to work with horses every day!

"I'll be back to get you in a couple of hours," her mother said. "Call me if you need to be picked up before then." She waved to Mrs. Miller, who sat on the front porch, then drove off.

On the way to the barn, Jordan stopped to admire the big bed of marigolds that she'd always viewed from the road. She heard giggling and turned to see to a splotch of blue disappear into the trees at the edge of the lawn. Daniel's siblings seemed to be doing their best to hide from her. She hoped they weren't watching her driving lessons.

She continued on to the barn and was totally unprepared for what she saw. Tommy Sutton stepped from the interior of the old wooden structure, pushing a wheelbarrow full of dirty straw. He hesitated when he saw her, then lowered his head and kept going.

Was *this* the surprise Jacob talked about?

"What are *you* doing here?" Jordan said with an accusing tone. She couldn't imagine what Tommy would be doing at the Miller farm. How had Jacob reacted when he saw him?

"None of your business what I'm doing here," Tommy snapped. He put the wheelbarrow down, eyeing her curiously. "What are *you* doing here? You're not hanging out with these throwbacks, are you?" When Jordan didn't say anything, his eyes widened. "You are, aren't you?" He hooted with laughter.

Jordan didn't see anything funny about that. Jacob and Daniel were a whole lot better to hang out with than he was. Why did kids always pick on anyone who seemed the least bit different?

Tommy emptied the wheelbarrow on the muck pile, then disappeared back into the barn.

Jordan stood there for a minute trying to decide if she should cut through the barn and risk seeing Tommy again or walk the long way around. She heard shouts coming from behind the barn and decided to take the outdoor route. She hoped Tommy hadn't provoked Jacob into a fight. The Amish and Mennonites believed in peaceful ways—but Tommy Sutton didn't. She broke into a jog and rounded the corner of the barn, then pulled to a stop at the scene before her.

Jacob had harnessed his horse to another Percheron and connected them to a couple of long poles that lay on the ground. He walked behind the team and to the side of the logs, guiding the horses through a series of cones.

This must be log skidding! Jordan couldn't believe her good fortune.

She watched as Jacob moved the horses—and the load they were pulling—in and out without disturbing the cones. A small crowd of men and boys who were probably waiting for their turns hollered in support as the horses and driver navigated the course.

So this is what all the commotion was about, Jordan thought as she joined the onlookers.

Unfortunately, when Jacob and his team rounded the orange cone at the top of the turn, they hit it with the edge of the log and knocked it several feet to the side.

"Awww," Jordan said in sympathy. She didn't know any of the rules for skidding, but she was pretty sure hitting a cone meant points off in a contest. Jacob managed the rest of the course with only a couple more penalties, then it was Dan's turn.

Mr. Miller motioned for Jordan to join them. She walked with him to where Jacob and his team stood and helped him unhook the large black horses from the logs so Daniel could hook up his team.

"This is so cool!" Jordan said.

"Yup. But it's hot work!" Jacob looked up at her briefly, then led the two horses to the water trough for a drink.

"This is a beautiful horse," Jordan said, petting the sweaty hide of King's pulling mate. "Where did he come from?"

"This is my dad's horse, Duke," he said as he watered off the horses. "This is the team I use when I compete in log skidding. They're a good team and I'm hoping to do well at the fair this year. The competition is only a couple months away." He tied the horses to a hitching post.

Jordan thought about her silly threat to beat Mr. Sutton. Jacob and Daniel had been doing this most of their lives, and she was only on her second driving lesson. She hoped the town grapevine wouldn't spread that little bit of gossip back to Mr. Sutton.

"So what's the deal with Tommy Sutton?" Jordan asked, following him to where all the others stood watching Daniel getting ready to run the course. "Why is he here?"

Jacob frowned and Jordan noticed he still had the ugly bruise on his forehead from the accident. "The kid driving the car was eighteen and has to stand trial," Jacob explained. "But Tommy got off with probation and a hundred hours of labor. The judge wanted to send him to Brother Fisher's place to work, but he thought it would be too disruptive to the Amish community."

"So he sent him here instead?" Jordan couldn't believe it. "Why?"

"Maybe so he'd learn tolerance and a little respect," Mr. Miller said as he helped Daniel secure the logs. He waved his son on and stood back under the shade of the barn. "That boy's doing a lot of hard labor and we appreciate the help, but I think maybe he needs us a whole lot more than we need him. He just doesn't know it yet." The men standing around him seemed to agree.

Jordan wasn't exactly sure what Mr. Miller had meant by that remark. But Daniel was starting the course, so she focused her attention on him.

He expertly drove his team and the heavy poles through the first several cones without mishap, but came close to touching on the fourth one.

Jordan stood mesmerized by the skillful coaching Daniel used with his team to pull the long poles in and out of the cones. She cheered with the others when he dragged the complete course with only two faults.

While they unhooked the big Belgians from the load, Jordan shared her news about Star Gazer.

"That's great!" Jacob gave her a pat on the back. "Then I guess we better make sure you're up to speed on driving horses by the time Star is ready to be harnessed."

Jordan's pulse raced at the thought. Jacob was right. She had a very short amount of time to soak up as much information and training as she could. Star Gazer had given up on pulling. It was Jordan's job to remind the mare how good she'd been—and how much fun it would be to work together as a team. And maybe if she could prove to her mother that she and Star Gazer made a great team, her mom would change her mind about selling the mare.

She rubbed her hands together. "I'm ready. Let's get started!"

sixteen

W hat's this?" Jordan asked, eyeing the beat-up old cart Candy was harnessed to. It looked like something her father had once built to pull behind his bicycle—only this one was a lot bigger. And uglier.

Mr. Miller hooked a lead line to Candy's bridle. "You did so well yesterday that I thought maybe we'd get you started on the training cart earlier than planned." He patted the bright red cushion.

Jordan looked at the cart doubtfully. She remembered seeing lots of nice carts parked inside the big barn. Where had this old thing come from?

"I wish you could see the look on your face right now," Jacob said. "You look like Cinderella when her coach turned back into a pumpkin."

Daniel laughed.

Mr. Miller motioned for Jordan to get into the cart and handed the lead line to Jacob. "Don't pay those two boys any mind, young lady. This is just our insurance policy against ruining a good cart. There are always accidents with a beginner," he said. "Once you can handle this cart, we'll let you drive one that's a little nicer."

The cart's two big wheels stood at least four feet high. It had to be tall to match the size of the draft horse and to allow the driver to see over its rump. Jordan managed to clamber in without losing her dignity. She quietly picked up the reins while Mr. Miller held Candy, waiting for Jordan to get ready.

"Just remember all of your lessons from yesterday," Mr. Miller said. "The cues are going to be exactly the same. You're just higher off the ground now, that's all. Jacob has a lead line on Candy, and he'll walk beside her to make sure nothing goes wrong."

Jordan took a deep breath. She could feel her hands shaking on the reins. "Walk up," Jordan said to the mare, but Candy didn't move. Jordan remembered the lecture Jacob had given her about Star Gazer not minding her. She sat up straighter and tried to make her voice sound more confident. "Walk up!" she said again, then shook the reins up and down and clucked.

Jacob pulled on the lead rope and stopped the horse.

"Uh-oh, I forgot and slapped the reins on her rump," Jordan said.

"But, you remembered. That's good," Jacob said. "I even heard a little more command in your voice when Candy wouldn't obey." He handed her a driving whip. "Use your voice to tell her you mean business," he instructed. "And if that doesn't work, tap her with this if she refuses your request."

Jordan frowned and declined the whip. "I don't like hitting a horse. It seems mean."

Daniel rolled his eyes. "I know," Jacob said. "My sister says the same thing. But it's only mean if you use it unfairly or with too much force. Don't think of it as a whip. Think of it as a tool to help you drive."

She still hesitated.

Jacob sighed. "Look, Jordie, say I was standing in line behind you and I needed you to move up. If I took one finger and put a little pressure in the middle of your back, you would move forward, right?"

Jordan nodded.

"And I wouldn't have to shove you or knock you down, right?"

"Right."

He smiled and handed her the driving whip. "Think of this as a finger poking Candy in the back. It doesn't have to hurt. It just reminds her to move forward, okay?"

Jordan took the whip, unsure how she should hold it. She already had her hands full of leather reins.

"This might take some getting used to," Jacob cautioned. "You're going to have to hold it in your right hand along with the reins."

Jordan rearranged the reins and whip, then signaled that she was ready to go. Jacob led Candy toward the paddock they'd worked in the day before.

Mr. Miller opened the gate. "We're going to start you here until you're used to the cart. Then we can move you out to the big pasture," he said. "Daniel set up some orange cones for you so you can practice turns."

Daniel poked Jacob in the ribs and a conspiratorial look passed between the two of them.

"What's with you guys?" Jordan asked, looking from one to the other. "Come on, out with it."

Jacob waited until the horse and cart passed through the gate, then he climbed up onto the bench seat with Jordan and settled in next to her. "Daniel bet me that you'd run over at least four cones..." He paused. "And I said you'd only run over three."

"What?" Jordan yelped. Everyone laughed and she joined

127

in. But part of her felt a little hurt that they didn't have more faith in her.

Mr. Miller closed the gate behind them. "Jacob is going to stay in the cart with you and give you direction. If you run into problems, he can take the reins for you."

Jordan watched as Candy's ears flicked back and forth, listening for a cue. For a split second, Jordan panicked. The horse was so big, and she was so small. But the moment passed and she picked up the reins. She had to learn the correct way to do things, for Star's benefit. The better she was able to work with Star, the better the chance of getting to keep her. Soon it could be Star Gazer's big rump she'd be trying to see over. The thought brought a big grin to her face.

* * *

An hour—and six smashed cones—later, Jordan had to admit that it was a lot more difficult than it looked. How did the boys manage to pull those long poles through all of those cones without disturbing them? She couldn't even make a turn around a cone with a whole paddock to do it in.

She walked Candy to the harnessing rack, removed her tack, and began to bathe her.

Mr. Miller patted Jordan on the back. "Don't look so down in the mouth, kid. You're doing just fine." He tipped his hat back and gave her a fatherly smile. "The wheels stayed on the buggy, and everything—including you—is in one piece. I'd say it's a good day."

Jordan had to agree when he put it that way. Daniel was lucky to have such a great dad. She couldn't help wondering what things would be like if her own father were still around.

She untied Candy to walk her to the pasture where her

teammate stood waiting. She stopped and turned back to Mr. Miller. "I really appreciate you working with me. I hope I can be a good horsewoman someday."

Mr. Miller handed her an apple to give to Candy. "I think you're going to be a fine horsewoman. We've got a lot of summer ahead of us, and the boys seem to enjoy teaching you. You're welcome to keep coming over if you want."

"That would be great," Jordan said. "I'd really like that." She held the apple out for Candy. Unlike Star, who took the entire apple in one bite, Candy took dainty little nibbles until it was gone. "Is there something I can do to help around here? You guys are spending a lot of time on me."

Mr. Miller removed his hat and scratched his head. "Well, I suppose you could fill water tanks. I've got the Sutton boy doing stalls."

Jordan had almost forgotten about Tommy. She'd seen him stop several times on his way back and forth to the manure pile to watch her driving lesson. She hoped he hadn't witnessed her running over the cones. She tugged on Candy's lead rope and walked her out to the pasture.

"In about ten minutes, Mrs. Miller has a treat for everyone," Mr. Miller called. "We'll meet in front of the barn."

Jordan put Candy to pasture and started on the water troughs while Daniel and Jacob cleaned tack. She dragged the hose to the first stall. As she filled the tank, she daydreamed about driving Star Gazer. She didn't look up until she heard the wheelbarrow roll by.

"Nice driving, McKenzie," Tommy said in his best sarcastic tone. "Only six cones down? Amazing. I'm really looking forward to watching you and that lame mare beat my dad in the pulling contest." He laughed all the way to the next stall.

Jordan gritted her teeth. Why did he have to rub it in? She

already felt self-conscious enough about her less than stellar horse skills and driving abilities. But then it occurred to her that Tommy wasn't exactly one to be talking about driving skills after the accident he and his friend had caused. She opened her mouth to speak, then hesitated.

Tommy frowned, staring at her like he could read her thoughts. "Go ahead. Say what you were thinking."

Jordan shook her head. She wasn't going to let Tommy bait her. But the smarmy look on his face pushed her over the edge. "I think you—"

"What's going on here?" Jacob interrupted the tongue-lashing she was about to give Tommy.

"Everything okay ?" he asked, walking straight for them. He looked first at Jordan, but his eyes came to rest on Tommy.

The Sutton boy puffed up his chest and stepped away from the wheelbarrow. "What? You going to beat me up if things aren't okay?"

"Give it a break, Tommy," Jacob said.

The boy gave a mean laugh. "Oh, that's right. You Amish boys don't like to fight." He moved a step closer.

When Jacob came forward, Tommy retreated a couple of steps. "It's not that I *won't* fight," Jacob said. "It's just that there's a better way. Don't confuse the two. And I'm *not* Amish."

Tommy stared at him for a few moments. "You sure dress like one." When Jacob didn't respond to the comment, Tommy snorted and pushed the wheelbarrow to a stall at the end of the aisle.

"Hey," Jordan called after him. "Mr. Miller wants everyone out front in ten minutes."

Tommy didn't even acknowledge her words. *Well, it's probably better if he doesn't come anyway.* Jordan thought. *I'll never understand that jerk.* She returned to her job filling the tank.

After Jacob left, Tommy rolled his wheelbarrow back to the stall next to Jordan. He set the cleaning fork down, then stood there staring at her, his mouth drawn into a hard line. Jordan felt her face flush and she looked away.

"Your watchdog isn't here now," Tommy said. "Why don't you go ahead and finish what you were going to say?"

Jordan thought about ignoring him, then she considered spraying him down with the hose she held in her hand. The thought made her grin.

"What are you smiling about?" Tommy said. "There's nothing funny here. I'm forced to work for a bunch of throwbacks who still plow their land with horses."

Jordan cocked her head, confused. "Your dad owns the biggest Percheron farm in the area."

"So? He also owns a brand new John Deere tractor. That's what we use to plow our fields—not stupid horses." Tommy picked up the cleaning fork. "I've got better things to do with my time than shoveling manure for these yahoos. Or talking to you." He marched off down the barn aisle, leaving the wheelbarrow sitting there.

"You really don't get it, do you?" she yelled at him. Her common sense told her to stop right there. Tommy came from the foremost family in town, and despite being such a jerk, he seemed to be popular. She was the new kid in town. If she made a total enemy of him, he could make her life miserable at school next fall.

Tommy looked back at her with total disdain, like *she* was the one who had done something wrong. He'd harmed her friends and her horse and it didn't seem to matter to him. Jordan decided she couldn't take it anymore.

"You did a really bad thing, Tommy," Jordan said, looking him right in the eye. "Don't you get it? People could have been killed in that accident." She pulled the hose out of the overflowing trough and kinked it. "Your friend is in jail because of what you guys did. I would think you'd be glad that you got off with an easy punishment like cleaning horse stalls."

Jordan walked past him to turn off the hose. Her hands shook so badly that she had trouble turning the shut-off valve. She stopped just outside the barn door and took three big calming breaths, then went up to the front lawn to wait with the others. Tommy Sutton was a hardheaded fool. She'd rather spend her time with good people.

Daniel's siblings were all there when she arrived. The two youngest kids ran and played tag, while Daniel's sister sat primly in a lawn chair. She was older than Jordan, but she spoke to her politely and made her feel welcome.

Mrs. Miller came through the front door with a big tray. Jacob and Daniel ran to help her. Jordan's mouth watered when she saw all the treats: cookies, sweet bread, watermelon slices, and a big pitcher of lemonade.

Mrs. Miller wore a plain, modest blue dress and a comfortable-looking pair of flat shoes. Her clothing reminded Jordan of photos she'd seen of her grandmother as a kid.

"It looks as if we're missing someone," Mrs. Miller said. She set down the tray and poured the lemonade into tall glasses. "Where's the Sutton boy?"

"Sulking in the barn," Jacob said through a big mouthful of sweet bread.

Jordan accepted a cold glass of lemonade and thanked Daniel's mother. "I told him we were meeting here. I guess he didn't want to come."

"If he doesn't want to come, let him stay where he is," Daniel said, taking a handful of butter cookies.

"Now, boys…" Mrs. Miller gave them a stern look. "It's not nice to think unkind thoughts." She glanced toward the barn, like she could see through it to where Tommy was sulking. "Perhaps someone should take him some food. He's worked hard today. Would you like to make him up a plate, Jordan?"

Not really, Jordan thought, but she nodded and filled one of the small paper plates with a sampling of the treats. She grabbed a napkin and headed for the barn.

"Jordan, wait," someone called.

When Jordan turned back, she was surprised to see Jacob striding toward her with a tall glass of lemonade in his hand. "What's up?" she asked.

Jacob handed her the glass and shrugged. "He might be a real pain, but Tommy worked pretty hard today. He's probably thirsty." He paused a moment. "Are you okay? Do you want me to go with you?"

Jordan shook her head and Jacob returned to his lawn chair.

She smiled to herself. Jacob seemed to practice what he preached. She wasn't sure she'd be so forgiving if Tommy had recklessly crashed into their car.

Inside the barn, the temperature was much cooler. Flies buzzed lazily and sparrows chirped in the rafters. Spotting the wheelbarrow at the end of the aisle, Jordan walked in that direction. She stopped outside the stall that Tommy was cleaning.

He paused with his pitchfork in midair. "What do *you* want?"

With that snarky tone in his voice, what Jordan wanted was to dump his cookies in the wheelbarrow and walk off. But she tried to follow Jacob's example and pasted a pleasant look on her face. "Mrs. Miller made some really good treats," she said, holding out the plate, "and she wanted to make sure you had some of them before the rest of the kids polished them off. Jacob poured you a glass of lemonade."

Tommy leaned the fork against the wall and stepped out into the aisle. "Oh, he did, did he?" He eyed the food suspiciously. "Well, I don't want it." He crossed his arms and glared at her.

Jordan sighed. "Tommy…"

"*Tommy*," he said, mimicking her in a whiny girl voice.

Jordan's shoulders slumped. "Why are you so mean?"

Tommy laughed, but it didn't sound friendly. "Hey, I'm shoveling manure for a bunch of people I don't like. It's hot out here, the flies are eating me alive, and you think I should be happy that you brought me a few cookies?"

"I think you don't see what is plainly in front of your eyes because you're too busy complaining," she said. "I think you need to get over yourself! *That's* what I think."

She turned and walked away, so upset that her hands were shaking. She almost dropped the plate of sweets, and her arm felt sticky from the lemonade that had sloshed over the rim of the glass. She should have known better than to even try with a knot-head like Tommy.

seventeen

Hey, McKenzie, wait up!" Tommy ran down the barn aisle after her. Jordan stopped, tears stinging the backs of her eyes. She didn't want this rotten guy to see her crying. She blinked back the tears and reluctantly turned to face him.

Tommy ran his hands nervously through his hair, then reached out for the plate and the glass of lemonade. He looked everywhere but directly at Jordan. "Thanks," he mumbled. "Tell Mrs. Miller and Jacob I said thanks." Without another word, he turned and strode away.

Astonished, Jordan stared at his retreating back. Guys could be so weird. Especially Tommy.

Shaking her head, she headed back to the group and relayed Tommy's message. Mrs. Miller smiled, but no one else said a word.

"Hey, Jordan, you have to keep up the driving lessons," Daniel said, breaking the silence. "Jacob is going to keep King and Duke here for a few weeks so we can practice log skidding. We're both going to enter the contest at the fair this year."

Jordan held back a sigh. These two boys were entering a contest that would take them up against the likes of Gilbert

Sutton and some very talented teams. And right now, it was all she could do to keep from running over the cones.

"I'll be rooting for you guys," Jordan told him. "Someday, after I get the hang of driving, I'd really like to learn how to skid."

Daniel grabbed another cookie from the tray. "Your mare was a decent skidding horse. I bet she'll come around again."

Mr. Miller joined them and poured the last of the lemonade into a glass. He polished it off in several big gulps. "As soon as Star is walking well enough to be worked lightly, I'll come get her in the trailer. We can rig some harness to fit her and see if we can get her interested in driving and skidding again."

Jordan wanted to jump out of her chair and shout "Yes!" She couldn't even imagine how much fun driving and skidding would be with Star Gazer. "That would be really cool, Mr. Miller." She forced herself to keep her voice calm. "Thanks for the offer," she said. "Star is walking better since you guys loaned us the boots, but it's going to be a while before she'll be able to do anything like pulling logs."

Jordan just hoped that she got to keep the mare long enough to be able to put her under harness.

The sound of a car horn alerted Jordan to her mom's arrival. Mrs. McKenzie stepped from the car and spent a few minutes talking with the Millers and thanking them for all their help. Jordan said her good-byes and got into the car, anxious to get home and check on Star.

As she backed out of the driveway, Jordan's mother told her about the vet's visit. "Dr. Smith just finished up with Star Gazer a little while ago," she told Jordan. "He drained the abscess in her foot and cleaned it out. He said we need to keep those boots on her and keep the abscess clean. If things go well, we should start to see a big improvement soon." She swept a loose strand of hair off her forehead. "You know, Jordan, these horses are a lot of work."

Her mother was right about that. Taking care of an animal was a big responsibility and a lot of work. But taking care of an injured, damaged animal was an even bigger responsibility—especially when the animal was as large as Star. But she was happy to do it.

Mrs. McKenzie reached over and turned down the volume on the radio. "Umm, Jordan…"

"What is it, Mom?" Jordan detected a trace of guilt in her mother's voice.

Mrs. McKenzie kept one hand on the steering wheel. Her other hand fidgeted nervously with the chain around her neck. "We've got a guest coming over shortly."

"A guest?" That got Jordan's attention. She hoped her mom hadn't done something crazy like invite Jacob over for dinner.

Mrs. McKenzie cleared her throat and began, "The other day, I put an ad for Star on the bulletin board at work. A lady called today, and she's coming over to see Star."

Jordan was stunned. *An ad for Star, and a lady was coming over to see her?* "See her for what?" Jordan asked, already knowing the answer.

"Jordan…," her mother sighed. "You know we have to sell Star Gazer. We've got to find a good home for her. This woman was interested in Star even though she knew there was a problem with her feet, so that tells me her heart is in the right place." She glanced at Jordan. "She lives in the next town over. You'll be able to stop in and see Star when you want."

Jordan felt like someone had punched her in the stomach.

She thought she was going to be sick. "You talk like it's already a done deal," she muttered. She felt confused. Betrayed.

When they pulled into their driveway, Jordan saw an old Chevy truck parked next to the house and a woman with a young boy and girl sitting on their steps. They stood and waved as the car came to a stop.

Mrs. McKenzie put the car in park and got out, motioning for Jordan to follow.

"Hello, Mrs. Cannon," Jordan's mom said. "This is my daughter, Jordan. She's the one who has been taking care of Star Gazer. Come to the barn with us and we'll be happy to show her to you."

The woman smiled broadly. Jordan attempted to smile back, but it came out as more of a grimace.

"I'm really excited about this," Mrs. Cannon said as she waved a well-manicured hand in the air. "I wanted a horse as a child, and my parents wouldn't get me one, so I'd like to give my kids an opportunity I didn't have. And, my husband thought having a horse in our field would cut down on all the grass mowing—especially a *big* horse. She'll eat more." Mrs. Cannon laughed at her own humor.

Star is going to be used as a lawn mower? Jordan felt her jaw drop and quickly snapped it closed.

As they walked down the hill to the barn, the young girl grabbed Jordan's hand and skipped beside her. The boy ran alongside them. Jordan's legs moved stiffly, like she was in a bad dream.

Star was out in her corral behind the barn. When the mare saw Jordan, she raised her head and trumpeted a welcome. It broke Jordan's heart to think that just as Star was beginning to get attached to her she might have to go live with this woman who cooed and held out her hand while clucking to her. It was clear that Mrs. Cannon had no idea that clucking meant "go" or "go faster," not "*come here.*"

Star limped over to the fence and poked her massive muzzle at Jordan, begging for a treat. "I'm sorry, girl," she said in a voice choked with sadness. "I don't have anything for you."

Mrs. Cannon produced a large carrot from her purse and held it out to Star, trying to coax her down to where she stood. Star flared her nostrils, taking in the scent of the treat, but she stayed where she was.

Jordan smiled inwardly and stroked the white star in the center of the mare's forehead. "What do you want to do with Star if you get her?" Jordan asked, curious as to what she had in mind. Surely she had a better purpose for Star than just being a glorified lawn mower. The lady didn't look like a horse person. She had long, painted fingernails, a fancy hairdo, and a roly-poly shape. Jordan doubted she'd ever been on the back of a horse.

Mrs. Cannon laughed. "I just want a pasture pet," she said. "Something we can play with and feed carrots to. Maybe sometimes we could toss the kids up on her back and lead her around a bit."

Jordan frowned. Star would need someone who could give her extra help, not somebody who knew little or nothing about horses. Jordan didn't consider herself fully competent, but this woman knew a lot less than she did.

Mrs. McKenzie turned to her daughter and smiled. "That sounds like a nice life, doesn't it, Jordan? Especially for a horse that's not very sound." Her mom searched her face, looking for some sign of approval.

"Mom," Jordan said, refusing to believe that her mother would make a mistake like this. "Star was a champion pulling mare. Her feet are going to get well again. She should be in front of crowds, showing off her strength and beauty, not tucked away in a pasture and forgotten." The thought made her really sad. Jordan felt a tear slip down her cheek. Star stuck her nose in Jordan's hair and let out a gentle *wuff,* making her feel even worse.

Jordan scratched Star behind the ears. The mare sighed contentedly and blew through her lips, then suddenly flinched and raised her head. "What's the matter, girl?" The big mare flinched again and sidestepped nervously.

Jordan heard a giggle and looked around. Mrs. Cannon's little boy had stuck a big stick through the fence and was poking Star with it. "Why you little…" Jordan glared at the boy and walked toward him. He stuck out his tongue at her, then tossed the stick and ran.

"Now, Anthony," Mrs. Cannon wheedled. When her son ignored her, she turned to Jordan. "You know how it is," she said with a laugh. "Boys will be boys."

Jordan found nothing the least bit funny about it. If Star went to live with this family, that little brat would make her life miserable. And Mrs. Cannon seemed to see nothing wrong with her child tormenting a horse.

"She's really beautiful," Mrs. Cannon said. "Of course I'll have to talk this over with my husband. And I'll need a couple of weeks to get our place ready. But I'm *very* interested in your horse."

Jordan felt her heart breaking wide open. She couldn't stand it any longer. She headed back toward the house, not bothering to say a word to anyone. She knew it was rude, but she didn't care. She went straight to her room, crawled into bed, and pulled the pillow over her head to shut the world out. She couldn't stop the tears this time.

A while later she heard a soft tap on her door. It was followed by the sound of footsteps coming across the room. She felt the mattress sink as her mom perched on the side of her bed. Jordan sniffed and took the pillow off her head. "Did she buy her?" She barely managed to choke out the words.

Mrs. McKenzie brushed the stray hairs from Jordan's wet face and handed her a tissue. "Not yet. She'll call us back when they've made up their minds."

"Star will be miserable there!" Jordan cried and fresh tears began to roll.

Her mother handed her another tissue. "Jordan, there are worse things than living on tall pasture and having someone feed you carrots all day. Star was on the way to the packing house when you bought her."

"That little boy will torture Star, Mom," Jordan said. "Didn't you see him poke her with that stick? She won't like living with them. Please don't sell Star to those people."

Mrs. McKenzie frowned. "Look, Jordan. Right now, they're the only buyers we've got. If you can find someone better, I'd be happy to see her go to a home that you approve of."

Jordan thought for a moment. If there was no way she could keep Star for herself, then she'd at least like to see her in a home with people who knew about horses and could take good care of her—a home where people would let her do what she was bred to do.

She sniffed, willing herself not to start crying again. "Mom, we can't let Star go to the Cannons' house. If you'll give me a little more time, I'll work with Star and get her pulling again. I'm sure Mr. Miller and the boys will help me."

Her mother raised a doubtful brow. "Are you sure this isn't an excuse to get more time with your horse?"

Jordan blew her nose and wiped her eyes. "You know I

want to spend as much time as I can with Star, but if we have to sell her, then I want her to go to the best place possible," Jordan reasoned. "If we can get her back to pulling again, then someone who knows what to do with her will buy her. At least that way Star would have a better life." She looked down at her hands. "Mrs. Cannon seemed to mean well, but I don't think she can provide the right home for Star...especially with that little monster kid around."

Her mother thought about it for a moment. "Okay, Jordan," she said. "You have a good point. And if you can get Star back into top shape, someone will pay more for her, and you can put that money back into your savings account. Mrs. Cannon said it would be a while before they can make an offer. That will buy you a little time."

"Thanks, Mom." Jordan still felt rotten about the prospect of Star leaving, but she had a mission now. Star had to be restored to a great pulling mare so she didn't end up as a pasture ornament—or worse, as a victim of that horrible Cannon boy.

* * *

Jordan spent the next several weeks learning everything she could about driving draft horses. Daniel, Jacob, and especially Mr. Miller were excellent teachers. They sympathized with her having to find Star a new home and promised to help as soon as Star Gazer was ready to work.

Tommy still gave Jordan a bad time about her driving skills, but she tried not to let it bother her. His time of community service for the Millers was almost up, and he wouldn't be around there much longer. Still, she could hardly wait for him to go. She was tired of hearing him brag how his dad was going to beat everyone at the log-skidding contest. He only boasted to her, never when they were within earshot of Jacob or Daniel.

One lazy sunny day, when Candy was behaving perfectly, Jordan begged Mr. Miller to let her take the mare for a few laps around the pen by herself while they went to harness the other horses. She wanted to prove to herself that she was good enough now to stand on her own. He agreed to a few extra minutes, so Jordan and Candy slowly plodded around the arena, enjoying the perfect day and the sense of freedom. Jordan tried to imagine what it would be like to drive Star like this.

Jordan was deep into her daydream when she heard something whiz through the air. Candy suddenly sparked to life, grabbed the bit in her teeth, and took off at a run.

Jordan's heart leapt into her throat, and she grabbed for the reins. The cart careened around the corner on one wheel. "Easy, easy!" she called to the runaway mare while she tried to get Candy back under control. They made three laps of the arena before Jordan was able to pull the horse to a stop.

Jordan sat in the cart, her hands trembling on the reins. A movement by the barn caught her eye, and she looked up to see Tommy standing there with his arms folded and a satisfied smirk on his face. He gave her a snappy salute before he turned and went back into the barn. Jordan had a feeling if she could search Tommy right then, she'd find a slingshot in his pocket.

She debated on telling Mr. Miller, but she knew she couldn't prove anything. Tommy would soon be gone anyway. She'd heard he was going to work at the feed store. His dad had probably pulled a few strings to get him that job. If he treated the customers the way he treated her, though, he wouldn't last long.

Jordan climbed down from the cart and secured the reins, then walked to the front to lead Candy by the bridle. The runaway incident had been scary, but it was most alarming to her that it had taken her so long to get things under control. Jordan realized that she was very lucky she hadn't been hurt.

She heaved a big sigh as she led Candy through the gate. She knew her horse skills were getting better—everyone but Tommy said so. But this accident really showed her just how much more skill it was going to take to keep a big draft horse under control. Once they got up a full head of steam, drafts were a force to reckon with and nothing like the small horses she had ridden in the past. Jordan thought about Star Gazer and her shoulders slumped when she realized she still had a long, long way to go.

eighteen

Between driving lessons and odd jobs, Jordan worked hard on Star's feet. The abscess finally healed, and with the daily regimen of hoof oil, vitamins, and good feed, Star's hooves were finally long enough. They called the farrier and had him put on the shoes.

A few days later, Jordan caught Star Gazer bucking and playing one evening when the weather was cooler. It was a good sign, and she liked seeing Star play. But part of her worried what would happen if the Percheron tried any of those rodeo antics when she rode or drove her. After the runaway accident with Candy, she had a newfound respect for the power these draft horses had.

Jordan had been trying hard not to let Star take advantage of her, but every now and then, the big mare took it into her head to do things her own way. And when that happened, Jordan couldn't stop her.

Jacob had explained it like this: "Horses in a herd have a pecking order and they all know what it is. The top horse bosses all those below him and the last horse gets bossed by everyone."

Right now, Jordan was at the bottom of the pecking order.

She was going to have to find a way to be the *top horse* in their little herd of two.

Dr. Smith stopped by to examine Star late one afternoon and declared her ready for light exercise. "Just be very careful with those feet, and keep her off the rocks and hard surfaces like pavement," he said. "This mare's doing great. We don't need a setback."

Jordan agreed. They'd worked too hard to have something go wrong now. Every night, after the hot Michigan summer air cooled, she and Nicole took their horses for walks by hand in the pastures surrounding Jordan's house.

Jordan even bought a long rope called a longe line so she could trot Star in a wide circle over the soft grass surface of the small side pasture. She tried it once in the big pasture, but Star Gazer pulled the rope out of her hands and took off to the other end of the field to graze. Jordan was scared to death that the one of the mare's hooves might hit a rock in her headlong flight, causing her to come up lame again. But fortunately Star wasn't injured. From then on, they worked in the small fenced-in pasture so the draft couldn't go far if she got away from Jordan.

Gradually, Star Gazer got used to the routine and she behaved much better, but Jordan couldn't help wondering how Star had come to have such disregard for minding her owner. To win pulling competitions, she had to have behaved well at one point. What had Tommy and his dad done to her in the last year she'd been on Sutton Farm?

As the days went by, Jordan grew restless with the walking routine. She dreamed of riding Star, and taking her to the Millers' place to begin driving her in a cart.

The morning the veterinarian finally pronounced Star sound enough for heavier exercise, Jordan went straight to the laundry room, where her mother was taking sheets out of the washer. "I think today's the day, Mom," Jordan said. "I want to ride Star Gazer."

Seeing the worried look on her mother's face, Jordan rushed on with her explanation. "It'll be fine, Mom. Nicole is coming over to help in about twenty minutes. You can stand by with your cell phone ready to dial 911 if it makes you feel better."

Jordan glanced at the clock on the wall. "I'm going down to brush Star now. Jacob loaned me one of their bridles."

Knowing how long her daughter had waited for this moment, and sensing that arguing would do no good, her mother just sighed. "What about a saddle?"

"Everyone says Karina rode her bareback," Jordan said. "Don't worry, Mom. I'll bail off at the first sign of trouble." She crossed her fingers and hoped it wouldn't come to that.

Her mother kissed her on the top of her head. "Better pack a parachute, honey. That's a long way down. As soon as I finish up here I'll be right down to help."

Jordan pulled on her riding boots and grabbed the helmet she'd purchased at a local garage sale. She couldn't shake the jittery feeling that had set in the moment the vet had proclaimed Star ready to ride. She'd waited for this moment for so long. She just hoped it would be everything she dreamed of, and not a disaster. What if Star decided not to cooperate? She took a deep breath and headed to the barn.

Star whinnied and bobbed her head when she saw her. "You're excited, too, aren't you girl?" Jordan readied the bridle and got out the brushes. As she groomed Star, she looked at her tall back. Getting up there was going to be a problem, but if she could coax her over to the haystack, it would just be a matter of sliding onto her back.

"Knock, knock." Nicole peeked through the barn door. "Are you ready to go?"

"I've still got to bridle her," Jordan answered. "And we've got to wait for my mom to get here. She's bringing her cell phone with 911 on speed dial." They laughed.

Jordan pulled the bridle off the hook and approached Star, not sure what to expect. If the mare raised her head to avoid the bit, that wouldn't be good. "Okay, girl, here we go." She held the leather headstall in her right hand and the bit in her left. For a moment Jordan had a feeling that Star was going to resist. Then the big mare lowered her head and twitched her lips, looking for the bit. "Good girl," Jordan crooned, slipping the bit into Star's mouth and pulling the bridle up over her ears.

She led Star out of the stall and over to the haystack in the middle of the yard. Nicole held Star's reins while Jordan climbed the haystack, preparing to mount. She took a moment to steady her nerves. She wasn't afraid of the mare— well, maybe just a little nervous. But she was really excited to finally be riding her.

When Nicole had Star in position, Jordan spoke softly to her horse and slipped her leg over her side, then settled onto her broad back. She sat up straight and marveled at the feel of being so far off the ground. This was even better than riding King. *This was her very own horse!*

Star shifted under her and Jordan felt her pulse quicken. She adjusted the leather reins in her shaky hands. *Relax*, she chided herself, remembering that several weeks ago she wasn't sure if Star would ever be able to walk without hurting herself. And now the mare was carrying a rider, waiting to go for a run!

"Well?" Nicole said. "Is it really cool?"

Jordan grinned. "It's really, *really* cool."

"Should I just let you go," Nicole asked, "or walk out with you?"

Jordan tensed her shoulders, then let them go. "Better stay with us until we get out of the yard and I feel a little more confident."

Just as Jordan slowly walked Star, her mom appeared. "Oh, my, you're already up," she said. "Are you okay? Wait, let me get a photo!"

Nicole and Jordan smiled for the camera. "Can I get Dakota and ride with you?" Nicole asked. "Or do you want me to keep walking beside you?"

"I think I'm okay now," Jordan replied. "I'll do a couple of circles while you get Dakota, just to make sure I've got good turns and stops."

Jordan's mom sucked in her breath. "Yes, please tell me you have brakes on that horse. Otherwise, it'll be like riding a tractor with no way to stop it."

"We'll be fine, Mom. You worry too much," she said. But the truth was, she was a bit worried herself. If Star decided to do things her way, there wasn't a lot Jordan could do. If she decided to run away to the other side of the field, like she had a few weeks ago when she was longeing her, it would be like sitting on a runaway freight train. It would be wiser to begin in the small, enclosed pasture.

Jordan asked Star Gazer to circle to the right. The mare pulled a little on the bit, but she made a good circle to the right and then to the left. She even stopped and backed up when asked. Jordan couldn't have been happier. No words could describe the feeling of sitting on top of such an awesome horse. Everything about a draft horse was bigger and better than those horses she'd ridden during her riding lessons in Los Angeles. She walked another circle, moving with the rocking motion of Star's steady gait.

Nicole mounted up and rode Dakota next to Star Gazer. The mare nickered to him and the two horses touched noses. Mrs. McKenzie opened the gate to the small pasture, still looking a bit cautious, and closed it behind them.

Jordan sat up straight and proud. After all the waiting and all the problems, she was finally riding Star Gazer!

* * *

After several successful rides, Jordan made plans with Mr. Miller about driving lessons for Star Gazer. He picked the mare up the following morning. Jordan was glad to have her off their property so Mrs. Cannon couldn't swing by and visit her whenever she wanted. The woman had called back twice to let them know she was still interested and to explain that building a shelter was taking longer than they had expected. Jordan was glad for the extra time.

When they arrived at the farm, Jacob and Daniel already had their horses harnessed. Candy and Suzie were hooked as a team, and King and Duke stood nearby in sturdy old harness. That meant Jacob planned to practice log skidding today.

Jacob came to help unload Star Gazer. "Heard you've been riding her," he said. "It's going to be another big day today when you get to drive her for the first time." He walked Star to the harnessing area.

Jordan practically skipped behind him. Just the thought of driving Star sent butterflies twirling around inside her stomach. The mare had been pretty good to ride so far, and her feet hadn't seemed to bother her. But several times Star had taken the bit in her teeth and walked to a tall patch of grass to munch. Jordan knew she needed better control, but she hadn't wanted to punish the mare so soon.

150

"Dan and I rigged some harness for you," Jacob said. "His dad had some old team harness sitting around gathering dust so we made it into a single for you. Wait here and keep Star company. I'll go get it."

He returned in a moment and placed the equipment on Star's broad back. Jordan helped him hook all the straps and straighten the harness, proud that she could now do this without making a mistake. When they were finished, Jacob handed her the reins. "Here's your horse. Back her out of here and we'll go to the front paddock. Mr. Miller set up some cones so you can practice."

"Great," Jordan muttered. More of the dreaded orange cones to run over. She fussed with the long driving reins, getting them set just right in her hands. The excess rein lay over her shoulder, arranged so she couldn't become entangled in it.

Jordan stared at the big backside of her horse. Star turned her head, trying to see around the leather pieces that sat at eye level on the bridle. Jordan was sorry they'd had to put blinders on Star, but she knew it was important to keep the horse focused just on what lay before her. Some horses spooked when they could look around at the scenery and the load they pulled, so blinders were standard on most harness.

Star hadn't shied at anything when she'd ridden her in the pasture. As soon as Jordan could afford to buy her own bridle, she'd get one without blinders.

"What are you waiting for?" Jacob asked.

"I don't know," she said, realizing that she'd been stalling. "I've waited a long time for this moment, and now that it's here…I guess I'm kind of nervous…maybe even a little scared."

Jacob's head snapped up in surprise. "Scared? But you've

been driving Candy for weeks, and you're doing well. What are you afraid of?"

Jordan shrugged, remembering the runaway disaster with Candy. She had decided not to tell anyone about that, but it lingered in the back of her mind. "Lots of things," she answered. "What if Star doesn't want to do it? What if I'm not good enough? She can be kind of headstrong sometimes. What if she drags me around like she does when I'm walking her?"

"I'll help you, Jordie," Jacob said with a sympathetic smile. "Back her out of here and I'll walk along beside Star until you're comfortable. She can't go very far in that paddock."

Jordan didn't find that very comforting. Candy hadn't been able to go very far either, but the speed they'd reached in that little paddock made it a Do Not Repeat event in her mind.

Jordan lifted the reins to back Star. The mare hesitated only a moment before she began to work her way backwards. She stopped when she stood free of the harnessing station.

Standing behind Star Gazer, Jordan pulled herself up tall. *This is it,* she thought as she readied the reins. *A million things could go wrong, but a million things could also go right.* She squared her shoulders, then smooched to Star and gave the command: "Walk up!"

nineteen

Star immediately started forward and Jordan's spirits soared. She took long steps to keep up with the mare's big walk as she guided her toward the paddock where they would work. She couldn't help but grin. Driving Star Gazer was so awesome!

Jacob opened the gate for her, and Jordan steered the big Percheron through the opening.

"Start her around the corner cones and practice keeping her on the outside fence, just like you do with Candy," he said. "Mr. Miller is coming to help. I'm going to go get some more cones."

Jordan guided Star over to the fence and made a lap clockwise around the paddock. A cone had been set in each corner, about ten feet off the fence line. The goal was to keep Star between the outside fence and the cones when going around the corners. She kept her hands light, like Mr. Miller had shown her, and kept a good feel on Star's mouth. Jacob had taught her to communicate with her horse not only by voice command, but also by contact with the bit.

Mr. Miller entered the paddock and stood in the middle. "This time around, I want you to do a complete circle of the cones when you reach each corner," he said. "Let's see what kind of steering power you have with this mare."

As they approached the first corner, Jordan thought about what she needed to do. *Envision the task you're going to perform before you get there so you know exactly what you need to do,* Jacob had told her during her first lesson. She went over the cues in her head.

As they walked into the corner, Jordan called out, "Star, come around, gee!" and gave a light pull on the right rein. Star bent her head to the right and made a circle around the cone, then went back on the rail and headed for the next one.

Jordan felt like she was walking on air when they finished the final cone. She pulled Star to a halt and rewarded her with the sound of her voice and a short rest. "Good girl!" she said, letting the reins go slack so the mare could relax.

Jacob entered the pen with an armload of the orange cones. "Great job!" he told Jordan. "Take it easy for a couple minutes while I set these up, then we're going to have some real fun!"

Jordan watched as Jacob reset the cones, this time in a straight line, many yards apart. Daniel joined his dad and the two of them jumped on the fence to watch.

"What's this?" Jordan asked, pointing to the line of cones down the center of the arena.

"This," Jacob said as he took the reins from her and got behind Star Gazer, "is the first step in learning to skid logs. Let's go."

"Really?" A nervous tingle ran down Jordan's arms. "But I'm not very good. I still run into things in the cart."

Everyone laughed. "You've got to start somewhere," Mr. Miller said. "We'll get you used to maneuvering around obstacles. By this time next year, you'll be entering that pulling contest and giving the boys a run for their money."

Jordan thought again about the challenge she'd laid out to Mr. Sutton. She shook her head at her stupidity.

Jacob stood several yards behind Star Gazer in the driver position. He motioned for Jordan to step in front of him, lifting one rein so she could slip between the two driving lines.

She moved into position between the driving lines—and also between Jacob's arms. Her heart rate kicked up a couple of beats.

"Put your hands lightly on the reins, Jordie," he said. "I'm going to run this course with Star, but I want you to feel what I'm doing with the reins and see how Star is moving her body. You just keep your hands lightly on the reins and let me do the work."

The sound of Jacob's deep, steady voice over her shoulder made it hard to concentrate. What was going on with her? Jacob was just a friend who happened to be a boy. Why was she so jumpy? She took a step forward to put a little space between them. It made breathing a little easier, and, she reasoned, they'd need the extra space so their feet didn't get all tangled together as they walked forward.

Jordan was glad Nicole wasn't here. Her friend would be making all kinds of monkey faces at her and shooting as many photos as she could to "capture the moment." Jordan didn't think she'd easily forget this moment for a long while.

Jacob gave Star the walk-up command, and Jordan prepared for the sudden jolt forward as the big mare strode forward. Jordan fell into the rhythm, feeling Jacob's big leather boots hit the ground just behind her. She kept her hands barely skimming the reins so she could feel what Jacob was doing without interfering in his communication to Star through the reins and bit.

It surprised her to see how differently Star responded to

the more experienced driver. The big mare moved forward confidently, picking her way in and out of the cones in a serpentine pattern, her ears swiveling back and forth to catch the sound of Jacob's voice. Jordan could feel the lightness of his touch and the steadiness of his hands. She wished she had his confidence and ability!

"See how Star kind of side-passes in and out of the cones while keeping a forward motion?" Jacob asked. "That's what you're going for. No big swings of movement, okay? You don't want your logs bouncing around and knocking things over when you're in a contest."

They finished the line of cones in one direction, then circled the end cone and headed back the other way. Jacob gave her control of the reins and joined the others on the fence. She could immediately feel the difference in the way Star responded. Jordan tried to do as Jacob had instructed, but her moves were awkward and Star swung wide on her passes through the cones. She even knocked a couple of them down.

Jordan frowned as she turned Star, determined to make another pass through the cones. But Star Gazer had other ideas. She grabbed the bit in her teeth and took Jordan to the outside fence, where she promptly stopped to rest. No amount of urging could encourage the horse to budge.

"What's she doing?" Jordan asked, annoyed and frustrated. "Why won't she go?"

Mr. Miller walked over and took Star by the bridle, leading her away from the fence. "Looks like this might have been what she was doing at the Sutton place. Sometimes horses figure out how to get out of work. Let me see her for just a minute." He took the reins from Jordan and steered the mare back to the course. Star tried to get out on him several times, but Mr. Miller was firm with her and guided her through the course.

When they finished, he signaled for Jacob. "Bring King in here, please. And, Daniel, go get the team driving lines. We're going to hook these two as a team and see if we can get Star to remember her manners."

"How will that help?" Jordan asked.

Mr. Miller smiled. "King is bigger than Star and outweighs her by a couple hundred pounds. He's also very good at obeying his driver. The next time Star tries to make up her own routine, King will hold her to the set course."

When Jacob brought King into the paddock, Star Gazer lifted her head and nickered a greeting. She stood quietly while Jacob and Daniel changed the equipment and hooked them together as a team. "Well, let's see how well they work together," Jacob said, taking up the reins. He drove them around the paddock several times, then motioned for Daniel to open the gate.

"Where are you going?" Jordan asked.

"If it's all right with you, I thought I'd hook them up to a set of logs and see how Star pulls. Is that okay?"

Jordan nodded vigorously. It was more than okay. She couldn't wait! Star's feet had been holding up well. This would be a good test to see how sound she'd be after a tougher workout. The load was heavy, but the soft dirt in the pulling field would be easy on Star Gazer's feet. Jordan ran ahead and opened the gate.

Jacob guided the horses into the back pasture where he and Dan always practiced log skidding. The poles were already attached to the long piece of equipment called the "evener," so he backed the horses into place just in front of the load. Star stood quietly with King while Jacob hooked the harness tugs to the doubletrees on the evener. After a quick check of the equipment, they were ready to go. When Jacob gave the command to pull, the big mare grunted and leaned into her collar, pulling the logs forward with King.

Jacob made a pass up and down through the cones. Several times Star tried to quit and leave the area, but King faithfully plodded onward, taking Star with him. "That's enough for today," Jacob said. "We don't want to put too much strain on Star's feet at first. We'll let her build up to heavier work." He held the horses still while Mr. Miller unhooked them from the load.

Jordan ran ahead to open the gate and followed them back to the harnessing station, where she helped untack the two horses. Sweat dotted Star's black coat. She'd need a bath before being put out to pasture with King.

Jacob pulled some carrot bits from his shirt pocket and offered them to the horses. He patted Star's thick neck. "She tried to quit on us a few times, but outside of that, she did pretty good today," he said. "When she dug in and started pulling her share of the load, I could tell she's really got a lot of potential."

Mr. Miller and Daniel gave each other a look, obviously agreeing with him.

Jacob fed the mare another piece of carrot. "If it's okay with you, Jordan, I'd like to work Star with King some more and see if we can get her up to speed."

Jordan felt a surge of relief. She was just a beginner. No way could she correct Star's bad habits at this point. "That would be great," she said. Star turned her head and nuzzled Jordan's cheek as if making an apology. Jordan rubbed the big white star in the center of the Percheron's broad forehead. "I know you don't mean to make me look bad," she said.

Mr. Miller placed the harness in the wheelbarrow to return it to the tack room. "Don't think you're going to get off easy just because Jacob will be driving your mare with King." "You'll still be warming her up and driving her single before Jacob takes over," he warned Jordan.

"And I'll let you step in and drive the two of them with me, just like you did when we started off today's lesson with Star," he added.

Jordan cheeks grew warm thinking about standing between Jacob's arms. It was totally unnerving.

Jacob handed her Star's lead rope. "Keep this up, and next season you might just be the first girl to win the pulling contest."

* * *

Jordan spent the next month in a constant state of busyness. When she wasn't mowing lawns, walking dogs, or pulling weeds, she was riding with Nicole or taking lessons at the Miller place. She'd even had a chance to ride to the lake with Mary and Kathy from the stable. Kathy made a snide remark about Star's size, but Jordan counteracted it by riding up beside Kathy and looking down at her shorter horse while they spoke. Jordan suspected that Kathy was secretly impressed with Star—maybe even a bit jealous.

Mrs. Cannon made an offer of five hundred dollars on Star, but Jordan's mother turned it down. Now that Star was showing a lot of potential, it was obvious they could get a better offer. Mrs. Cannon wasn't giving up, though. She said they'd look at their finances and see if they could come up with a little more money.

Star Gazer loved getting out and doing things, but she still had a mind of her own. One day when the mare decided to take Jordan on a detour, Nicole showed Jordan a secret.

"Pull on that rein and make her turn in a tight circle!" Nicole hollered when Star tried to wander off the trail. "My trainer tells us that horses don't like doing extra work, especially small circles," Nicole said. "Star has to follow where her nose goes, so pull on that rein and tip her nose to the inside. She'll have to follow and that will keep her from getting her own way."

Jordan tried it several times and it seemed to work. It was difficult for a horse as big as Star Gazer to move in a tight, nose-to-tail circle. After a while, Star gave up trying to get her way—most of the time. There were still moments when Star got the drop on Jordan and moved like a bulldozer, plowing toward a big clump of sweet Michigan grass. But things were getting better and Jordan was feeling more confident. She vowed to remember Nicole's trainer's theory: "Make the right things easy and the bad things difficult."

Lessons at the Miller place had really intensified since Jacob and Daniel both planned to enter the pulling contest at the fair at the end of the month. Jordan worked hard, too, and she loved every minute of it. Her dream was finally coming true.

On lesson days, Jordan drove Star to warm her up, and to get in some driving practice. Under Jacob's competent hands, Star Gazer worked well. She wasn't able to pull her tricks on him. It amazed Jordan that Jacob could get those two big draft horses and the logs through the obstacle course without knocking down any cones.

He let her drive the pair for a short time each session, even helping Jordan work them through the log-skidding course. At first Jordan had to pick up a lot of tipped-over cones when they were through, but as summer wore on, she knocked over fewer and fewer of them.

Now and then, Jordan would see Tommy Sutton standing across the street watching her and the boys practice. She wondered if maybe he wanted to hang out with them, but he never got close enough to talk to them. Once when she waved, he picked up his bike and rode away.

Jordan got to the point where she didn't feel quite so self-conscious about having people watch her. She even relented and invited her mother to come watch. She didn't even complain when her mom took tons of photographs. Her mother seemed to be thrilled with their progress. Several times Jordan caught her looking at Star Gazer with new respect.

After the photo session, Mrs. McKenzie stood by the fence with Jacob, watching Jordan guide the mare through a series of cones. "They make a good team," Mrs. McKenzie said.

"I keep trying to tell her that she's doing well, but she doesn't want to believe me," Jacob said.

When Jordan finished the lesson, she came to join Jacob and her mother at the fence.

"Are you sure you don't want to enter the contest yourself?" Jacob asked her. "There's a category for beginners. You can use a single horse and pull just a single log. You're doing really well, and Star Gazer's feet are holding up just fine. I think you should enter. It would be a good experience."

"And it will give people a chance to get a good look at Star," her mother added. "It might make it easier to find a good buyer."

In her mind's eye, Jordan could see Star taking off for the outside of the arena and the whole crowd laughing at her. "Thanks, but no thanks," she told Jacob with a laugh. "Not yet, anyway." She turned Star toward the barn and motioned for her mom to follow them.

But as Jordan led Star Gazer through the gate, the idea of entering her horse in the beginner's class and competing with the other kids in town suddenly seemed less scary.

She tied Star to the hitching post and pulled the reins from the guide rings on the harness. She knew her mom was dead set on selling Star Gazer. But maybe if she could keep the mare in line and do well in the beginner's class at the fair, her mom would see what a great team they made and let her keep her.

twenty

Mrs. McKenzie went to sit on the porch with Mrs. Miller while Jordan helped the boys put the horses away. When Star was bathed and brushed and fed, Jordan signaled to her mother that she was ready to leave. They said good-bye to their friends and climbed into the car. Her mom had promised to take her to the feed store today. Star needed vitamins and Jordan wanted to get some more horse cookies. The mare loved the oats and molasses treats.

Jordan rolled down the window, letting the wind blow in her face. After making such a big deal about *not* entering the contest, she had to figure a way to tell her mom that she'd changed her mind. Also, money was tight and they'd have to come up with the entry fee. She rolled the window back up and squirmed in her seat, trying to rearrange the seatbelt on her shoulder.

Her mother glanced at her while she waited to pull onto the main road. "You're awfully fidgety. Is everything okay? Did something go wrong with your lesson? It looked to me like things were going well."

Jordan cleared her throat. "Mom…I've been thinking about that beginner's class Jacob talked about. I think maybe it wouldn't be so bad to enter Star Gazer at the fair this summer. That is, if we haven't sold her by then," she added with a frown.

"I don't know if that would be a good idea, Jordan," her mother said. "Star still likes to disobey you occasionally and take you to the outside fence. If we're trying to sell her, it might not be good to have potential buyers see that. Let me think about it." Her mother was silent all the way to the feed store.

As they slowed to make the turn into the parking lot, Mrs. McKenzie took up the conversation again. "You know, if you do have a good showing, it might help us find a good home for Star. It would be nice if she went to someone local here so you could go visit. But still, if anything went wrong…"

Jordan turned her head to look out the window. She didn't want her mom to see the tears gathering her eyes. It wasn't fair that she'd spent the whole summer working with Star Gazer just to turn her over to someone else. Couldn't her mom see how much she loved that horse?

As they pulled into a parking space, Jordan saw the Sutton Farm truck and cringed. She hadn't even thought about the possibility that Tommy would be working. She would hurry. Maybe they could get in and out without seeing either Tommy or his dad.

When Jordan opened the door, the first thing she heard was Mr. Sutton's voice booming out, bragging to others in the shop that he would win the big pulling contest again this year. Didn't he ever get tired of bragging about the same thing? *He might not be talking so big after the competition,* Jordan thought, *if Jacob and Daniel have anything to do with it.*

When her mother stopped to scratch the ears of the store cat sunning itself in the front window, Jordan slipped behind a big shelf in the vitamin section, trying to make herself as small as possible.

Jordan spotted Tommy stacking salt blocks in the back corner. He had his back to her. She quickly picked out some vitamins and found Star's favorite horse cookies. She had almost made it to the counter when Tommy spotted her.

"Hey, McKenzie!" His snarky voice carried across the feed store. "Kill any more of those orange cones lately? I hear they're on the endangered species list because of you." As usual, he seemed to get a kick out of his own attempt at humor.

"Who're you talking to, Tommy?" Mr. Sutton asked. Just then, he rounded the vitamin aisle and saw Jordan. "Ah, it's the new girl." He gave her a patronizing grin. "How's that mare doing? Did you get her feet squared away? My son tells me that you've been harnessing her and doing a little pulling?"

Jordan wished she could fade into the walls. She was sure Mr. Sutton remembered her challenge to him on the pulling contest. She was going to have to eat a little crow here, and the feathers were going to stick in her throat. She was about to answer when her mother joined them.

"Well, hello, Mr. Sutton," Mrs. McKenzie said with a smile that didn't quite reach her eyes.

Jordan looked back and forth between her mother and Mr. Sutton, hoping this didn't get ugly and embarrass them both. But her mother seemed calm.

"I hear Jacob Yoder and Daniel Miller have a very good team of horses this year," Mrs. McKenzie said. "There's speculation going around that you could get beat." The smile on her face tightened. A few other people in the store chuckled.

"Ha!" Tommy snorted. "It's going to be a blow-out this year. Nobody can beat my dad."

Mrs. McKenzie took the vitamins and horse cookies from Jordan and gave Tommy and his dad a contemptuous glare. "Oh, and by the way," she said. "In case you didn't hear, my daughter will be entering Star Gazer in the beginner's class. I hope you'll both be there to cheer them on." She turned on her heel and walked toward the checkout counter, leaving Tommy and his dad—as well as Jordan—staring after her.

Jordan came to her senses and hurried after her mother. She could feel Tommy's eyes burning a hole in her back. They paid for their purchases and left. Jordan waited until they got in the car, then turned to her mother. "Mom...you just told them I was entering that class. I know I said I wanted to do it, but I hadn't totally made up my mind yet. You know that now I'm going to *have* to compete, don't you?"

Her mother smiled sheepishly and put the car into gear. "I'm really sorry about that, honey, but I couldn't stand listening to the two of them shooting their mouths off." She reached over and patted Jordan's arm. "We're in this together now. If you truly don't want to compete, I'm fine with that. You don't have to enter that competition. But if you're still game, I'll back you and Star Gazer one-hundred percent. I'm really proud of everything you've done. You deserve this chance to prove yourself."

Jordan thought for a moment. Her mother was right. She and Star deserved this chance. She hurried to answer before her mother could change her mind again. "We've come this far," she said. "I guess we might as well just go for it."

* * *

The week before the fair was a busy one. Nicole came over to help every day, and Jordan's mom showed up twice to help clean harness and groom horses.

166

Jordan's hard work with Star over the past couple of weeks was beginning to show results. When they got into a battle of wills, Jordan had refused to let Star Gazer bully her like she used to, and her strictness was paying off. They'd only made two trips to the outside fence lately.

A couple of days before the big contest, Jordan decided to take the day off from the rigors of training and have some fun and relaxation. She joined Nicole for a ride to the lake. They packed sandwiches and sodas and set off for the one-mile ride to the small lake. It was a popular hangout for all the kids—especially now that it wouldn't be long before they'd all be back in school.

At the beginning of the summer, someone had put up a couple of small corrals under a large maple tree at the lake. Jordan and Nicole turned their horses loose in one of them. Jordan recognized Kathy and Mary's horses in the other one.

"Hurry up!" Nicole said as she ran across the short sandy beach toward the water.

Jordan placed Star's bridle and their lunch on a stump near the pen. "I'm coming," she replied. "Just hold on a minute. I want to make sure the ants don't get our lunch."

When Jordan got to the lake, Nicole had waded in up to her waist. "Come on," she taunted. "It seems cold at first, but it's fine after you get in." Mary and Kathy were sitting on the dock on their beach towels. Jordan ran past them and jumped in, creating a huge splash that totally soaked Nicole.

Her friend screeched like a banshee and splashed Jordan, and Jordan retaliated by pushing her friend under the water. They both came up sputtering and laughing.

A familiar voice sounded from the shore. "Hey, McKenzie! You look like a drowned rat!" It was followed by hoots of laughter from several boys Jordan had seen around town.

"Great," she muttered under her breath. Tommy Sutton.

"I can't seem to get away from that loser," she told Nicole.

"Just ignore him," Nicole said. "He'll get bored soon and leave."

But the boys had found a beach ball someone had lost in the weeds, and they took up a game of catch, trying to show off for all the girls.

Nicole brushed her wet hair off her face. "If I didn't know any better, I'd swear Tommy has a crush on you. Every time he makes a good catch, he looks over to see if you're watching."

"No way," Jordan said.

"Don't be so sure," Nicole said. "You said you've seen him stop by the Miller place to watch you drive Star."

Jordan frowned. "Don't even go there, Nicole," she warned. "If that's how Tommy treats someone he likes, I'd really hate to see how he treats his enemies."

Kathy was listening from her perch on the dock. "Don't flatter yourself, girls. Tommy's showing off for me. Everyone knows he's had a crush on me since kindergarten."

"You're welcome to him," Jordan said.

"What's all that commotion over at the horse pen?" Nicole asked suddenly.

Jordan looked up in time to see their horses rushing through the open gate. The boys grabbed the beach ball and jumped out of the way of the charging horses.

"Oh, no!" Jordan cried, splashing out of the lake. "Whoa!" she yelled at the top of her lungs. But neither of the horses paid any attention. They had their tails in the air and were heading toward home.

Nicole caught up and stopped beside her, water dripping into the sand under her feet. "How did they get loose?"

They turned to stare at Tommy. "He did it on purpose,"

Jordan said, wondering how anyone could be so rotten. "He knows I've got a competition in three days and he's trying to wreck it for me." Jordan thought about the paved and gravel roads Star would be traveling over on her way home. *With her bad feet...*

"Tommy Sutton!" Nicole hollered. "You're to blame for this mess!"

Tommy spread his hands in an I'm-innocent gesture. "I didn't do anything," he said. "Honest." He turned to Jordan. "Really, Jordan. I didn't do it."

Jordan dismissed him with a wave of her hand. "Whatever." Who knew if he was telling the truth? She turned to Nicole. "Can you call my mom to come get us?"

Nicole pulled her cell phone from her bag, punched in the number, and waited for the phone to ring. She listened for several seconds. "Your mom's not picking up. I'll try my mom, but I think she's at a doctor's appointment. Let's start walking."

They put on their shoes and gathered their things, then started up the long winding path to the roadway. Jordan went over things in her mind. Did she forget to latch the gate after they'd put the horses in? With the way Nicole had hurried her, it was possible, but she just didn't know. Her foot kicked something hard and she looked down to see what it was. "Oh, no," Jordan said. She bent to pick it up.

"What is it?" Nicole asked.

Jordan held up the large horseshoe that Star had torn off when she hightailed it home. The mare was going to run all the way home without one of her shoes. "This isn't good," she said, knowing that was the understatement of the year. If Star ran on the pavement and gravel all the way home, she'd be lucky to still be walking by the time she got there.

* * *

Jordan's mom pulled over to the side of the road, gravel flying and brakes screeching. The car came to a stop and Mrs. McKenzie jumped out of the car. "Are you girls okay?" She grabbed each of them and looked them over to see if they were harmed. "The horses came tearing into the yard with no riders," she said, panic still in her voice. "I just knew I'd find you lying in a ditch someplace bleeding. What happened?" She herded them into the car and pulled back onto the road. "Nicole, please call your mother and let her know I have you both. I ran off and left my cell phone on the counter."

While Nicole called, Jordan told her mom the story and showed her Star Gazer's shoe. "Was she limping?" she asked, sick at heart to think that all their hard work could go right down the drain from this one incident. Again she thought back to when they first got to the lake and tried to remember if she had latched the gate to the corral. Was all of this her fault? It would be so much easier to blame it on Tommy.

"I don't think she was limping," her mother replied. "Or, at least it wasn't so bad that I noticed it, but we better call the shoer, just in case. And maybe the vet."

An hour later, Mr. Walter was tacking the shoe back onto Star Gazer's hoof. "It could have been a lot worse," he told Jordan. "She must have run most of the way in the grass. Her hoof wall stayed intact, but she's a little ouchy on the foot right now."

"Should I pull her from the competition?" Jordan asked. She didn't want to hurt Star any more than the race home had already done.

Mr. Walter tapped in the last nail and set Star Gazer's foot down. "I think she'll be fine," he said. "Just imagine if you ran home with one shoe on and the other barefoot. She might be a little tender for a day or two, so don't do any work with her over the next few days."

"What about pulling a load?" Jordan asked. "I've got the competition on Saturday. Won't pulling put an extra strain on her feet?"

"It might," said the shoer. "If you want to be totally safe, take it really easy on her. Maybe do just one class. Any more than that and you might risk laming her up again."

"I'm only entered in one class, so we should be okay," Jordan said. She thanked the shoer then went to the house to call Jacob and let him know she couldn't work Star Gazer again until the day of the competition.

twenty-one

The morning of the fair, Jordan got up extra early and fed and groomed Star. Mr. Miller would be over to pick them up soon. Jordan had butterflies so bad she couldn't even eat her breakfast, but Star chowed right through hers.

To make things worse, Mrs. Cannon had dropped by the house last night, letting them know that she planned to make a good offer on Star right after the competition. Jordan guessed the woman wanted to see if Star did well before she decided how much to offer. A poor showing would mean a cheaper deal for the Cannons.

When the Millers' big white trailer pulled into their driveway, Jordan and Star were ready to go. Her mother ran out of the house with her lunch and promised to pick up Nicole and meet her at the fairgrounds in an hour. Jordan loaded her horse and hopped into the pickup with Daniel and his dad.

"Jacob's going to meet us at the fairgrounds," Daniel said. "Duke didn't finish all of his dinner last night and Jacob is a little worried. But I think King's pulling mate just senses something is up. He's a little excited, is all. Some horses get real antsy about competition."

Mr. Miller looked over his shoulder and grinned. "So do some young men."

Jordan's brows rose. "You mean Daniel?" She looked at her friend. "*You* get competition jitters?"

Daniel nodded.

"But you're always so calm and steady when you work with the horses," she said. "Who would have guessed?" When Daniel didn't answer, Jordan looked out the window, but she didn't really see the passing scenery. She was too busy worrying. She hoped Duke was okay.

As soon as they pulled onto the fairgrounds, Jordan's pulse quickened. It reminded her of the day she went to the auction where she bought Star Gazer. People walked back and forth with their horses, and occasionally someone passed by with a sheep or goat for the 4-H competition. The carnival rides were already in full swing and she could smell cotton candy and popcorn on the air. After no breakfast, the sweet smells made her stomach ache.

Jacob was already there grooming King and Duke when they arrived at the barn. "How's Duke?" Jordan asked. "Dan said he didn't finish his dinner."

"I'm not sure," Jacob said. "He doesn't want his breakfast, either. I'm going to finish brushing them, then let them settle in. We've got another hour before we have to start tacking up. How's Star Gazer doing after that run from the lake?"

"She seems to be okay," Jordan said. "The vet came out yesterday and said her feet look fine. But he agreed with the shoer that I should take it easy with her for a bit. He said I could enter that one class today and that's it."

Jordan went to get Star's hay net and hung it in the corner of the stall. The mare immediately dug into her food. Jordan laughed. "Nothing wrong with *your* appetite." She settled into the straw in the corner and watched her horse eat, listening to the comforting sounds of Star chewing her hay and flicking her tail.

After a while, Jordan stood and brushed the straw from her jeans. She ran her hand over Star's sleek neck. "We've got to do well today, girl," she said, feeling her throat tighten with emotion. "This might be our last chance to work as a team." Star Gazer lowered her head and nuzzled Jordan's shoulder. Jordan threw her arms around Star Gazer's neck and buried her face in her mane. She couldn't keep the image of Mrs. Cannon driving away with Star out of her mind. She pulled back and looked Star in the face. "If we can pull this off and do well, then maybe a miracle will happen and I'll prove to my mom that we belong together. I can't lose you, girl."

Someone cleared their throat in the aisleway, and Jordan's head snapped around. Her jaw dropped when she saw Tommy standing there. He had heard every word she'd said.

"Come on, McKenzie," he said, shaking his head. "You know that horse can't understand a word you say."

"What are *you* doing here?" Jordan said, fighting the urge to pick up a brush and hurl it at him.

"Hey, I come in peace," Tommy said. "I just wanted to wish you luck. I feel kinda bad about what happened the other day. That was a pretty rotten break."

Jordan just stared at him. She still wasn't sure that she hadn't left the gate unlocked herself, so there wasn't much she could say.

"My dad's still going to whup your two throwback boyfriends in the main competition," he said. "But I think you'll do okay in your beginner's class. See you around, city girl."

Jordan watched him go, not sure what to think about the odd visit. She hugged Star Gazer one more time, then went to wait for her mom and Nicole. They walked around the fair for a bit, but Jordan's mind was too preoccupied to enjoy the exhibits. She finally told them she was going back to prepare Star for her class. Nicole offered to help, but Jordan said she wanted a little alone time with her horse. It might be her last chance. Nicole understood and gave her a big hug.

Jordan gathered her brushes and entered Star Gazer's stall. She began with the rubber curry, running it over Star's shiny, black coat. The mare cocked a back leg and wiggled her lips to show Jordan how much she appreciated the grooming.

When she was finished with the brushes, Jordan got out the hoof pick and made sure that Star's feet didn't have any stones or packed dirt in them. The shoer and Dr. Smith had cautioned her to enter Star in only one class because of her feet. Jordan wanted to make sure Star didn't come up lame before they made it to that one class.

Jacob showed up a few minutes later with the harness and helped her tack Star Gazer. Jordan thought he looked great in his jeans and plain blue shirt with black suspenders. It didn't matter that other kids made fun of him and Daniel. They'd both been true friends and she was happy she'd met them.

"This is your big moment," Jacob said, giving her an encouraging smile. "I'm really glad you decided to enter this class. You've earned the right to take your place in that competition arena. Just remember to take your time and go steady. No big moves."

Jordan smiled back. She could do this. "Whether we do well or really mess it up...," she said, hesitating for a second.

"I...I just wanted you to know that Star and I appreciate all your help. You've really been a good friend."

Jacob gave her the same lopsided grin she remembered from the first time she met him. He led Star Gazer out of the stall for her. "My team is already outside," he said. "Follow me out and we'll go practice in the warm-up arena. Dan and Mr. Miller are already there."

Jordan's mom and Nicole made it back just as they were moving the horses to the practice arena. Her mother immediately started snapping photos.

Star whinnied a greeting to King when she saw him. He bobbed his head and nickered back. Duke just plodded along beside King as they entered the arena. Jordan didn't like the dullness of his eyes or his listless appearance. The horse was off, and she knew Jacob was wondering how it would affect their overall performance.

Jacob motioned for Jordan to pull her horse alongside his. "I'm going to make a few rounds of the ring to warm these guys up," he said. "Then I'm going to put them in their stalls and come back and get you ready for your first time in the competition arena."

Jordan's stomach dropped at the mention of her first competition, and all her doubts came flooding back. Her hands shook on the reins. Sensing her nervousness, Star fussed at the bit and bobbed her head.

Jordan caught sight of Gilbert Sutton and his team of perfect Percherons warming up. As they approached each other in the ring, Jordan noted that Star looked every bit as good as Sutton's horses. She saw his eyes widen when he spotted them. He gave her a curt nod as they passed.

Jordan stood up a little straighter and squared her shoulders. She and Star *did* belong in the competition arena. They'd earned the right to strut their stuff. This was the day she'd prove to everyone that she and Star Gazer could do this!

Jacob signaled that he was leaving the practice area and would be right back. But ten minutes later, he still hadn't come to get her. The time for her class was quickly approaching and her knees were beginning to shake.

Mrs. Cannon appeared at the side of the practice ring with her husband and their two kids, waving wildly. Jordan forced a smile and waved back. Little Anthony kicked at the dirt, seeing how far he could make the clods and stones fly. Jordan gave him a look that made him stop immediately.

A small commotion caught Jordan's attention, and she spied Nicole running across the ring. The look on her friend's face told her something was wrong. Jordan pulled Star Gazer off to the side and waited.

"Duke's got colic and Jacob has to pull his team from the competition," Nicole said. "He's really bummed. Daniel will be out in a minute to help you. Jacob has to deal with the vet."

"Oh, no," Jordan said, feeling sorry for her friend. "That's terrible." Jacob had worked so hard to prepare his team. Jordan was sure he could have beat Sutton this year.

Daniel found them and motioned for Jordan to bring Star Gazer over. "It's time to get you to the holding area for your competition," he said. He pulled out a rub rag and flicked it over Star's coat to bring out the shine. After making a few last-minute adjustments to the equipment, he led them out of the ring.

Jordan exited the arena, but she shook her head when he pointed the way to the holding pen.

"You're not getting cold feet, are you?" Daniel asked, concern etched on his boyish face.

"Nope," Jordan said as she drove Star Gazer straight toward the barn. Daniel and Nicole hurried along after her, trying to figure out what she was doing. Her mother and Mr. Miller looked up in confusion when she entered the barn.

"We were just getting ready to go to the show ring to watch you," her mother said.

Jordan saw Jacob walking Duke up and down the aisle, trying to keep the horse's upset stomach from getting worse. "What are you doing here?" Jacob asked. "Your class enters the arena in ten minutes. You can't quit now. You've worked too hard for this."

"I'm not quitting," Jordan said as she led Star into her stall and removed her harness.

"Then what are you doing?" Jacob asked. He looked at her like she'd lost her mind.

"I'm loaning you my horse," Jordan said. "Star Gazer and King pull really well together. I want all of you to beat Gilbert Sutton."

Mr. Miller gave her an approving nod and turned to his son. "Daniel, could you run to the judge's stand and tell them there's been a switch in the team? Give them Star's name so they can substitute her in for Duke."

"But you worked so hard for this," Jacob said to Jordan. "This is your chance to prove yourself and Star."

Jordan reached up and lovingly straightened Star Gazer's forelock and gave the mare a kiss on her whiskered muzzle. "I think we've proved ourselves to everyone who really counts." She handed Star's reins to Jacob and took Duke's lead rope in return. "*You* can prove Star Gazer to the town. Now hurry up and get the horses harnessed. I'll get my chance at it next year."

Jordan took over walking Duke slowly up and down the aisle while the others worked to get the new team ready to go.

Mrs. McKenzie approached her daughter, being careful

not to get in the way of the big draft horse with the colic problem. "Dr. Smith is on the way," she said. "He's going to walk Duke for you so you can watch Jacob and Star compete. Nicole and I are going to our seats. We'll meet you there."

A few minutes later the veterinarian arrived. Jordan handed Duke over to him and ran to the arena. It didn't take her long to find their seats.

"Daniel goes first." Mrs. McKenzie pointed to where Daniel and his team stood in front of the set of logs. "The announcer explained that competitors are allowed to have someone help hook the load, so his father is out there with him."

Jordan watched Daniel move his horses into position. He looked nervous and out of sorts to her, not his usual steady self. When the logs were hooked, she heard him shout, "Candy, Suzie, walk up!"

The team moved toward the first set of obstacles. They made a good pass, but on the second set Jordan thought the team went a little wide. Daniel looked behind him as he walked, keeping a steady eye on the load to make sure the logs were skidding where he wanted them.

The crowd uttered a collective *"Oh!"* when one of the poles hit a marker and moved it several inches. Daniel made it through the rest of that pass okay, but after he turned his team to make the final run back through, he hit two more markers before reaching the finish line.

Jordan felt badly for Daniel. Nerves must have gotten the best of him. He'd had many perfect runs in the field at his farm.

They sat back and watched a few more teamsters compete, but those men had even more faults than Daniel. It reminded Jordan of just how tough this competition really was.

The spectators suddenly got to their feet and applauded. Jordan craned her neck to see what was happening and spotted Mr. Sutton driving his team up to the set of logs. She leaned forward to get a better view. He was supposed to be the best of the best. And although she didn't like the man, she could probably learn a lot by watching him.

Mr. Sutton gave his team of Percherons the cue to begin, and Jordan watched in reluctant admiration as the man made the entire run with only one small fault at the end. He was in the lead now. Jacob was the last competitor of the day and he had his work cut out for him. She looked over to where he stood waiting for his turn. He pulled the hat from his head and smoothed his hair. Jordan knew he was thinking the same thing she was: Sutton would be almost impossible to beat

"Jacob's up now," Nicole said, clapping along with the crowd. "And Star looks great!""

Too nervous to speak, Jordan watched her friend position Star and King for the hooking of the load. The horses looked every bit as beautiful as Sutton's team had. She leaned forward to get a better view and held her breath, waiting for the command to start.

"King, Star…walk up!" Jacob called to his team.

The horses leaned into their collars and strained to get the load moving. There was a moment of hesitation when Jordan was sure Star was going to pull for the outside fence, but Jacob steadied his lines and guided the horses toward the markers.

Jordan's heart pounded in her chest. She gripped the seat in front of her as she watched every move Jacob and his team made. Jacob kept his eye on the horses and the logs, calculating the movement of the poles as they went. The crowd let out an enthusiastic yell when the team completed the first pass and made the turn to come back through the markers.

Star's ears swiveled, and Jordan sucked in her breath as the evener at the back of the harness rigging started to rotate, meaning one horse was pulling more than the other.

"Star, no!" she cried as she saw the telltale sign: Star Gazer was contemplating a run to the outside fence. She felt light-headed and forced herself to breathe deeply again.

Jacob hollered to his team and made a quick correction on the reins, forcing Star Gazer back in line with King. The horses strained with the weight of the logs and made it past the first marker and onto the next.

The crowd got on its feet, cheering wildly. Jacob was almost to the end of the markers and he hadn't hit a single one of them yet.

Jordan stood up and cheered with the crowd, urging King and Star on to a clean finish. When they passed the finish line, Jacob's dad ran to help him unhook the team. Mr. Yoder patted his son on the back, and Jacob waved to the crowd as they shouted their approval.

"It looks like we've got our only clean round," the announcer told the crowd. "But give the judges a moment to compare notes and make a decision. While we're waiting, I need all contestants to move to the center of the arena, please."

It took several minutes for the competitors to line their horses up. Jordan nibbled her nails while she waited to hear if the judges had seen something that the crowd might not have. After a few more minutes, the judge entered the ring with an armful of colorful ribbons and a large trophy.

The microphone crackled as the announcer prepared to call the places. "In fifth place we have Daniel Miller." The crowd clapped as the judge stepped forward and awarded Daniel a fifth-place ribbon. The boy smiled and held the ribbon in the air, then moved his team out of the arena. Third and fourth places went to people Jordan didn't know. The crowd quieted for the calling of the last two ribbons.

"I'd like everyone to give a round of applause for all our competitors," the announcer said. He waited until the noise died down, then continued. "As many of you know, Gilbert Sutton has been our Log Pulling Champion for the past four years in a row and he's done a fine job again this time around." The crowd applauded and whistled.

Jordan's heart sank. Did that mean the judges had found a mistake on Jacob's part? Had he hit a marker that the crowd couldn't see and Sutton had won again? Nicole reached over and squeezed her hand.

The announcer continued. "But our first place trophy this year goes to Jacob Yoder, who guided his team to a faultless run and turned in a time five seconds faster than Sutton Farm's team."

Jordan let out a whoop of glee, jumping up and down and hugging her mom and Nicole. "They did it!" she cried.

Mr. Sutton accepted his second-place ribbon and Jordan didn't think he looked too happy about it. But he stepped over and shook Jacob's hand before leaving the arena.

Jacob's dad joined him in the arena and accepted the trophy for his son while the first-place ribbon was attached to Star Gazer's bridle. The crowd rose and let out another deafening cheer.

"Jacob Yoder…" The announcer dragged out the name, making it sound like an echo. "Take your team for a victory lap!"

Jordan's heart swelled with pride as she watched Star

Gazer and King move out confidently in a high-stepping trot while Jacob ran behind them, guiding them around the ring.

When they completed the lap, Jacob brought his team to the center of the arena and lined up beside the others. Star and King pawed the ground and shook their heavy manes, eager to be off again.

Mrs. McKenzie turned to Jordan and gave her an approving look. "That was a really nice thing you did for Jacob," she said. "I'm very proud of you. I wasn't so sure about things when you first brought Star Gazer home. But you've done a lot of growing up since then, and you've worked really hard. I think that maybe we just might keep that lovable ol' fuzz ball."

"You mean it, Mom?" Jordan couldn't believe her ears.

Mrs. McKenzie nodded. "Unless Mrs. Cannon comes up with an offer we absolutely can't refuse," she teased. "We do have your college fund to think about."

Everyone laughed and Jordan grinned broadly. "If it means keeping Star Gazer, I'll shovel a gazillion driveways to pay for college."

"I'll hold you to that," her mother said.

As they made their way down to the arena, Jordan connected eyes with Jacob and he waved for her to join him.

"Hurry up, you guys," Jacob called. "The photographer is waiting!"

He slapped Jordan a high-five when she reached him, then he handed her the reins to the winning team. At Jordan's puzzled look, he explained. "You saved the day, Jordie. If it hadn't been for you, I wouldn't be standing here with a blue ribbon right now. This belongs to you just as much as it does me. After the photo, I want you to take your own victory lap with Star Gazer and King."

Jordan smiled so big, her cheeks hurt. As she looked at the crowd, she wondered why she had thought it so important to prove herself to all of them. The people who really counted were right here in the photo with her.

They posed for the camera, then Jordan asked Mr. Miller to hold the reins for a moment while she walked to the front of the team and took Star Gazer's proud head in her hands. The mare lowered her muzzle so Jordan could plant a big kiss on it. "Next year," Jordan promised. "We'll get our chance at competition. But for now, let's show 'em what we've got."

Jordan gathered the reins from Mr. Miller and took her position behind the team. "King! Star!" she shouted to be heard above the roar of the crowd. "Trot up!"

author's note

K nown for their large size, kind temperament, and steady ways, the draft horse has a proud history dating back hundreds of years.

Through the centuries, the draft has been a war horse, a carriage horse, a freight puller, an artillery/gun horse, and a steadfast plow horse that has helped farmers feed nations. While today drafts can be seen in horse shows or on the trails, they are also still used as the main source of tilling the land in Amish Country in the Midwest.

The draft horse is gifted with a wide body, deep chest, thick powerful neck, large muscled hindquarters, and short powerful legs.

Chris Platt and her draft horse Celah

Despite their short legs, the draft is a tall horse, usually standing between 16 to 18 hands high at the withers. (A "hand" is 4 inches, a measurement derived from the average width of a human hand. "Withers" refers to the ridge between a horse's shoulder bones.) The tallest drafts have been measured between 19 and 21 hands. An average draft horse can range between 1600 and 2200 pounds, with some smaller breeds weighing less, and other larger breeds weighing more.

Information regarding some of the most popular breeds of draft horses can be found at the following websites:

The Percheron Horse Association of America
www.percheronhorse.org

The Belgian Draft Horse Corp of America
www.belgiancorp.com

Clydesdale Breeders of the USA
www.clydsesusa.com

The American Shire Horse Association
www.shirehorse.com

about the author

CHRIS PLATT has been riding horses since she was two years old. At the age of sixteen, she earned her first gallop license at a racetrack in Salem, Oregon. Several years later, she became one of the first women jockeys in that state. Chris has also trained Arabian endurance horses and driven draft horses. After earning a journalism degree from the University of Nevada in Reno, she decided to combine her love of horses with her writing. Chris lives in Nevada with her husband, six horses, three cats, a parrot, and a potbellied pig. Her previous books include the award-winning MOON SHADOW, STORM CHASER, WILLOW KING, ASTRA, RACE THE WIND, and many books in the popular THOROUGHBRED series. Visit *chrisplattbooks.com* for more information.

HORSE

TITLES

from *Chris Platt*

"Combining a hardworking heroine, supportive and loving secondary characters...
Platt creates a heartwarming, wish-come-true story." —*School Library Journal* (in review of MOON SHADOW)

MOON SHADOW HC: 978-1-56145-382-5 / PB: 978-1-56145-546-1
A young girl's love for a beautiful Mustang mare fuels her fierce determination
to save the life--against all odds--of the wild horse's orphaned filly.

STORM CHASER HC: 978-1-56145-496-9
Hoping to become a great horse trainer someday like her father and brother,
Jessica feels justified in working with the wild Storm Chaser behind her father's
back. But, after an unexpected disaster at the ranch,
going against the rules brings a heavy price...

ASTRA HC: 978-1-56145-541-6
Lily's passion is Arabian horses. Someday she wants to be a great endurance rider
like her mother. But a year earlier, when a freak riding accident took her mother's life,
Lily's father forbade her to ride ever again. Lily is determined to fulfill her mother's dream.
But how will she convince her father to let her ride again?

WILLOW KING PB: 978-1-56145-549-2
Inspired by the true experiences of a real championship racehorse, this moving story
celebrates the power of caring and the rewards of hard work.

STAR GAZER HC: 978-1-56145-596-6
When Jordan and her new friend attend the local auction, she sees a beautiful draft horse
about to be sold to the packers. Without her mom's permission, she spends all her money
to save the lame mare. She brings Star Gazer home, determined to restore her health and
help her become the champion she once was.

PEACHTREE ☥ PUBLISHERS
www.peachtree-online.com   (800) 241-0113 • (404) 876-8761